Copyright © 2022 E S Monk

Published 2022

ISBN 9798361764853

The Captain's Horses

By

E.S. Monk

For Ma and Pa

Sarah

Sarah felt the metallic taste of her own blood seep into her mouth. She hadn't even heard him coming. Sometimes he was like that. He liked to take her by surprise, a sort of one-upmanship in a game that only he wanted to play, a game filled with rules that only he knew. And sometimes, he liked to face her head on so he could see the fire of fear ignite in her eyes and watch her shrink before him.

Her head thumped from the direct blow, but the blood was of her own making. The sheer force caused her to bite down hard on her tongue in shock before crumpling to the floor. His face distorted with anger and malice. *How did I ever find him attractive?* she asked herself, as he stood over her. She had no time to answer her own question, though. In a split second, he was leaning forward, and taking a firm grip of her shirt collar, he roughly hauled her to her feet. Slamming her against the wall, her already aching head took another blow from the force of his manhandling. He was so close to her, she could see the light beads of sweat forming on his brow from the exertion of heaving her around like a rag doll.

Sarah stayed quiet. He was yet to enlighten her as to what she had done this time, and she had learned that talking too soon would only provoke him further. He liked to make her wait, to make her acknowledge his power. Only he knew what she had done, and he liked to enjoy the moment while she was still ignorant, still yet to find out. And she would only find out when he chose to tell her.

"You're late," he eventually snarled at her, punching the wall millimeters from her head, the enjoyment at seeing her flinch showing clearly through his steely eyes. She wasn't late. She was never late. But his rules and regulations changed on a whim, just like his own erratic behaviour.

"I'm sorry," she stuttered. Now that she knew her misdemeanour, she could figure out her tactics for placating him.

"Where have you been?" he barked at her, his hand pulling at her shirt collar, forcing it to tighten around her neck.

"The bus was late," she gasped. His strengthening grip was causing her to become breathless. And it had been. But she still hadn't been late. Whatever time he told her to be home, she was always, without fail, at least an hour early. She never took chances with the local bus service, never risked arriving home in the nick of time.

"Liar," he growled. "You've been talking with those women again, and that interfering bitch, Kelly."

"I promise you I haven't. I didn't see anyone at the yard today," Sarah said softly. "I went straight there, fed Gulliver, and came straight home again. I'm sorry I was late. Next time I'll make sure to get the earlier bus so I get home on time." She was trying desperately to calm him down and diffuse the situation.

She felt his grip slacken, allowing oxygen to fill her lungs. His temperamental outburst was over. Just like that, like a switch had been flipped, his clenched jaw and strained muscles loosened and his domineering persona vanished.

"I'm hungry," he announced. "What's for dinner?"

Without making eye contact, Sarah scurried into the kitchen to dish up the casserole she had put in the slow cooker that morning. After she had served up his generous portion, his curt voice cut through the air. "You're probably tired after your busy day. You go to bed, I'll eat on my own this evening."

Busy? she thought. *When am I every busy?* Her days were spent cleaning a house that was already immaculately clean, washing and ironing his clothes, preparing his meals, and on a good day, she was allowed out to run an errand for him. Her only saving grace was the two hours freedom he permitted her to see Gulliver, and even that was for his own ends. But she knew the game was up. She had been dismissed, and the punishment for her alleged tardiness was to go without dinner that evening.

Alone in the bathroom, she soaked her flannel in cold water before gently pressing it against her head. The thumping inside her skull was yet to subside and she knew when her eyes opened first thing the following morning, after a night like tonight, the usual persistent dull ache would accompany her for the rest of the day. The icy water brought a modicum of relief from the acute throbbing and the chilly droplets made her shiver when they landed on her bare skin. And then her stomach growled in frustration. No food, yet again. Another of his tricks. The more he starved her, the weaker she grew, and the more power he held.

He did the food shopping. That way, he knew each and every food item that was brought into their home, and if anything was taken. The beating she had received after 'stealing' food was one that she would never forget. The unrelenting hunger pangs on days he chose to starve her where nothing compared to what he would do to her if she took food from his kitchen. Even a single biscuit would be noticed.

Sarah filled a glass with the ice-cold water from the bathroom tap, glugged it down quickly, then repeated the process a second time. She had learnt to fill her stomach with water on nights like this, and all she could do was hope that tomorrow, her placemat at the table would be set alongside his.

Placing her third glass of water on her bed side table, she slipped her pale pink nightdress on over her head, pulled back the covers and eased herself into bed. *How did I ever end up like this?* It was a question she asked herself time and time again and would continue to ask herself until she did something to change her current solitary, enclosed, drudgery of an existence.

"Nineteen years," she quietly said out loud. In some ways it felt like her life had passed her by in the blink of an eye. But at the same time, her monotonous daily routine, interrupted with bursts of fear and pain, seemed like a lifetime prison sentence. Except prisoners didn't actually serve a lifetime in prison. They served their time and then were released back into the real world. They moved on even more quickly if they ticked every box on the good behaviour list. *But there is no such list for me.* She closed her eyes and pictured the day she first met him. Julian. Her husband and her tormentor.

A tall, slim, toned, charismatic young man had greeted her when she was working at a riding school all those years ago. He was out on a stag do with four other equally handsome, charming men. The stag, a keen rider, had organised for them to enjoy an hour's ride, followed by a pub lunch, before the real festivities began later that evening. Sarah had been their guide and had thoroughly enjoyed joining in with their happy banter and quick-witted jokes. Only the stag had previous riding experience, but Sarah knew how reliable the riding school horses were, and, when faced with the bravado of the young men, she gave in and permitted them a steady canter across the open fields, much to their delight. All five men thoroughly enjoyed themselves, as evidenced by their cowboy style yells of 'Yee Ha!' and the inevitable male competitiveness. Sarah had to admit that they were proving to be great company and she felt lucky to have been put on the rota as their guide.

Sarah was tending to the horses outside the pub whilst the men tucked into a hearty lunch and much needed pint, when one of the groomsmen appeared at her side with a crisp, cold pint of larger for her.

"From all of us," he had said to her. He offered her the pint, before introducing himself. "I'm Julian."

 She was smitten with him at the beginning. His golden hair, all messed up from wearing his riding hat, gave him a boyish charm, and his confidence and hilarious quips during the ride made him irresistible to the twenty-three year old Sarah.

"You're a fantastic rider," he had continued, then pointed at Gulliver. "This one is a beauty. Could I ride him back to the stables?"

Gulliver always stood out from the riding school horses, and Julian was not the first overly enthusiastic client to ask to ride him. And nor would he be the last. Gulliver was a 15.2, grey Andalusian gelding, and he was in a class of his own, especially compared to the ordinary, albeit lovely-mannered and even-tempered yard horses he was standing next to. As much as Sarah enjoyed receiving compliments about her beautiful horse, the answer was always no. No one was allowed to ride her Gulliver, not even the other experienced girls at the yard.

"His name is Gulliver," she replied proudly, "but I'm afraid he's not for clients. He belongs to me, not the stables, so unfortunately he's not insured for visitors to ride."

He had pushed, repeating his request, and charming her with his winning smile and clever retorts. *I should have realised then how much he liked to get his own way*, she thought ruefully as she remembered that first time she'd met him. He had masked it so well at the beginning. She really didn't have a clue as to what he was really like. The darkness was not revealed until after he placed the ring on her finger. And even then, he dripped his toxic malice out so slowly over the years. He had done it so cleverly that she didn't realise what he was doing until he had her hook, line and sinker, powerless to resist him. And she clearly recalled his disarming and shrewd tactics to try and manipulate her into riding her horse.

But when it came to Gulliver, no one could change her mind, not even the handsome stranger, and eventually, he gave in, but not before proffering more flattery upon her and winning her phone number. Sarah had been on cloud nine during the whole ride home, enjoying the secret smiles shared between them both and the anticipation of the promised phone call that was to come. And it did, two days later. Sarah remembered the elation she felt on hearing his voice at the other end of the phone, asking if she would like to go to dinner with him the following weekend.

How many times she had thought back to that one singular memory, the time when it had all begun. If only she had said no. How different her life could have been now. That one fateful meeting had changed her life forever. Even back then, the enigmatic Julian knew exactly what he was doing when he snared the naive, innocent young woman that she was.

"Enough," she told herself. There was no point going over and over what had been. She couldn't change the past. Reminiscing only resulted in upsetting her more, and tonight, like every other night, she was worn out with it all. She forced herself to block him from her thoughts, to be grateful for what she did have. For the only thing in her life that he hadn't ruined or taken from her. Gulliver. She pictured him in her mind's eye, his elegant grey face looking back at her with his gentle, kind, liquid brown eyes. In her imagination, she could feel the softness of his fur, the warmth of his breath on her fingers, and inhaling deeply, she could smell his sweet horsey smell, as if he was right there with her. She finally drifted off to sleep, knowing that tomorrow, she would be with him again.

Henry

Henry took refuge from the sweltering Canary Islands sun in the privacy of his air-conditioned cabin. Closing his door to signal he was not to be disturbed, he wiped the sweat off his brow before opening his private fridge and pulling out an ice-cold ginger beer. Settling himself at his desk, he took a refreshing swig of his drink, and accepted that he could put it off no longer. He tore open the letter bearing the handwriting he had come to know so well over the past six years.

Dear Henry,

I hope this letter finds you well and that you are enjoying the beautiful weather wherever you are. I am sorry how we left things when you were last on leave, and I am sorry that we did not part on good terms. I never wanted that. Nor did I intend to give you such an ultimatum. My feelings got the better of me in the heat of the moment, and I could no longer keep them to myself, not for a minute longer. I have loved you since the moment I met you, and I thought it would be enough, but as the years have passed by, I can no longer bear being alone for so many months at a time. I miss the daily companionship of a normal relationship. I miss having someone here, with me, when days are difficult, and the nights are long. And I yearn to share the good times, the little things that make my own life enjoyable. The things that we should share together privately as a couple. We do not have that, Henry. How can we possibly have that when we are parted for such lengthy periods of time?

It was wrong of me to ask you to choose between me and your life at sea. You would not be you if you could not board your ship and set sail to foreign lands. Your exciting, remarkable life is what drew me to you in the first place. Your stories of far-off exotic lands and all of the adventures that you lead. But it has also led to our demise. I am not part of your world, nor will I ever be. If I were to let you choose me, you would be like a caged bird, and we all know that the only song a caged bird sings is a haunting lullaby. You would end up resenting me, and so, after many days of consideration, I believe it best for us to part as friends, now, rather than wait for either me to resent your choice to continue your life at sea, or you to resent me for my request to choose me.

I will never forget you and I will always be grateful for the years we shared.

Goodbye, Henry.

With love, Louisa.

Henry stood up, retrieved the whiskey bottle from his cabinet and poured a generous glug into his ginger beer, grateful that his ship was docked, and three quiet days stretched out ahead of him before his ship would be loaded with shipping containers again, and they would set sail for Morocco. He stared blankly at her letter. His mind whirled with guilty relief, disappointment, and sadness. He was forty-five years old, and his life had been dedicated to the sea.

Leaving school at seventeen, he signed up to join the Merchant Navy, and on that day, he felt like his life had finally begun. And like any young man destined for a life of globe-trotting and adventure, the idea of settling down and finding a wife was very far from his thoughts. His long years at sea, coupled with his hard work and dedicated studying, had kept him focused and busy for twenty years, and then his day finally came. He could remember being on leave in Liverpool, sitting with his mother at her kitchen table, his results clenched in his trembling hands. He had done it. All those years of rising through the ranks culminated in ten full length days of examinations at the Merchant Naval University in Cheshire. And there, in his hands, was the piece of paper he had dreamed of receiving on the day he signed up to join the Navy, stating in black and white that he was a master mariner.

The lads he had joined up with and made friends with over the years had all had the same dream. But life sometimes got in the way, and it was not an achievable feat for everyone. They had dropped off one by one, either leaving the Navy or settling for their current rank, the thought of continuing the hard slog of university and many years working at sea becoming too much. But he had not lost focus on his prize, and he had not let anything distract him from his goal. Sharing his achievement with his mother, he could see the pride in her eyes. Her son was now at the penultimate step of the very high ladder he had been climbing since he was a boy. His results came with a letter containing a job offer. It was all very well passing his examinations, but he could not claim that elusive title Captain, until he had been commissioned to captain his own ship. The final step to climb.

He was to meet a ship in two days' time at Liverpool dock yard. A refrigerator ship, her name was Turicia, and he would be taking her to Jacksonville in Florida. And when he set foot on her, his name would finally be Captain Henry Hyam. His mother had starched his new white shirt to within an inch of its life and brushed his new doeskin captain's uniform to immaculate perfection. She accompanied him to the dockyard, and he felt such pride, having her on his arm as he led her up the gang plank, up the six flights of steps to his cabin, the captain's cabin. He closed the door behind them for privacy, wanting that moment to be shared only with her, the woman who had relentlessly supported him with his dream, and she enveloped him in her arms. He could still smell her familiar perfume and feel the gentle weight of her small frame holding him.

That had been the last time he saw her. Two weeks later, when he was in the middle of the North Atlantic Ocean, she had collapsed. An undiagnosed bleed on her brain had caused a fatal stroke. Amidst the heartache and grief of losing his beloved mother, Henry was so very grateful to have shared that wonderful, perfect day with her. He knew how proud she had felt accompanying him to his ship, and how proud she felt gossiping with her friends that her son, her Henry, was now a captain in the merchant navy. Henry was glad that he at least had been able to give her that.

His cabin felt stifling as his trip down memory lane began to suffocate him. "Enough," he said out loud. Opening his door, he stepped into the corridor and swiftly glided down the six flights of stairs. He slipped outside and inhaled the fresh air deeply. The scorching sun was beginning to set, taking its intense heat with it, and the light sea breeze offered a cooling relief. Henry headed for the gangplank. However, his hopes for an evening stroll were quickly dashed. As soon as he left the confines of the dockyard, he realised that the island of Tenerife was swarming with visitors. Each street and alleyway he turned down was heaving with cheerful holiday makers, their laughter and merriment filling the air. He couldn't stand it. Claustrophobia engulfed him and he made a bee line for a lone taxi, waiting patiently for a potential customer.

"Where would you like to go?" the polite driver asked.

"Anywhere away from here," replied Henry, then acknowledging his curt tone, he continued.

"Somewhere quiet, please."

The taxi driver gave him a kind, knowing look, before replying, "I know just the place."

Henry climbed into the back of the taxi and allowed the driver to whisk him away from the overbearing hustle and bustle. The driver remained quiet, providing a much-needed sanctuary in his silent car. Henry watched the concrete holiday resorts drift away as they headed north along the picturesque coastal road.

"Candelaria," announced the driver, as he weaved the car through the narrow streets of the small Canarian village. "Follow the road that way," he instructed, pointing down the steep road, "then turn right. A very different type of tourist visits here. Candelaria has deep-rooted religious connections and is more of a pilgrimage destination than a place for boozy night life!" He said with a a wry smile. "It is the home of our Lady of Candelaria," he explained. "Although popular with tourists in the daytime, the evenings are quiet and calm. I think you will find some peace here," he finished, with another of his knowing looks.

"Thank you," replied Henry, handing over the fee for his ride, then he watched the taxi driver head back to the hubbub of the tourist centre.

Henry did as instructed, and on reaching the end of the steep alleyway, he stepped onto the quiet main street of the little town. Boutique religious and tourist shops lined the street, now closed after the onslaught of tourists had returned to their holiday villages. The only people to be seen were locals, sitting outside with a drink after their busy day's work. They chatted contentedly in their native Spanish tongue, enjoying the warmth from the evening sun. Henry smiled and nodded as he strolled on by.

To his left, he spotted steps down to the sea. As he diverted towards them, he felt the sudden strength of the wind. The north-eastern village was exposed to the typical Canarian winds, and the narrow steps between the large buildings created a wind tunnel. Continuing down the steps, he reached the ocean, the waves crashing against the bottom step. Amidst the blustering warm air, and untameable waves, Henry closed his eyes, and for the first time since opening Louisa's letter, he felt a calmness envelop him. There was something about this place. He couldn't put his finger on it, but something in the air began to settle his whirling mind and calm his restless soul.

Retracing his steps back up to the street, he continued on his quest for inner tranquillity. The traditional square revealed itself before him. On his righthand side, there was a café. Although closed now, he could picture it filled with customers enjoying delicious food whilst taking in the spectacular view opposite them, of the ocean, stretching out as far as the eye could see, and the nine intriguing, beautiful statues, representing the aboriginal Guanche kings, standing guard and protecting the Lady of Candelaria. The statues stood tall and proud, lining the coastal wall opposite. And straight ahead of him was the Basilica.

Henry was not a religious man, but the enchanting village of Candelaria, with its mysterious spiritual atmosphere, encouraged him to set foot inside the highly-valued religious refuge. It was the main temple within all the Canary Islands, dedicated to the Virgin Mary, and many a pilgrim's destination.

The heavy wooden door creaked when Henry pushed it open. He stepped into the silent serenity of the Basilica. Detailed, colourful murals lined the walls and ceilings, and straight ahead, by the altar, was an intricately detailed statue of the lady herself. Sitting down on one of the hard, wooden pews, alone with his thoughts, Henry let the stillness engulf him.

It wasn't fair on her, he thought. *Mum had just died and without realising it, I used her to help me get through my grief. A distraction. Yes, a very enjoyable distraction, but that was what she was. Why did I not ask her to marry me? We both knew that was where we should have been headed, but I couldn't. Why did I allow it to continue for so long?* Round and round the questions went in his head as he tried to reason with himself over his own actions, but, when it came down to it, he realised that she just wasn't the one. He finally admitted it to himself. He had tried to love her enough, and he had tried to picture a life without the sea, but he couldn't. And deep down he knew that if someone really loved him for himself, for who he really was, they would never ask him to be something that he was not. They would never ask him to give up his life at sea.

Sadness seeped through him at the loss of Louisa. He would miss her. She had become a dear friend over the years, and he would miss the many letters she would send him whilst he was away from her. But that was not enough to string her along with the hope of marriage and a quiet life together ashore. Deep down he was grateful for her letter. She had been brave. Strong enough to call their relationship out for what it was and save him the heartache of admitting the truth to himself first. *Decent to the core, she is,* he thought genuinely. *She has taken responsibility and put an end to our relationship now. I will always look back on her fondly and be thankful we have parted as friends.* And Henry knew that was the best possible way.

Henry felt like a weight had been lifted after finally facing up to what his relationship with Louisa really was, and as guilty as it made him feel in that very moment, he was free. No relationship, no ties, no commitments to anything other than his work and his ship, and right now, deep down, he knew that is all he wanted.

He looked up and caught the eye of the Lady statue, and he nodded. It was his gesture of acknowledging her help, and his appreciation of the captivating mystery of her home. Religious or not, he sensed an age-old wisdom and peacefulness within her home, and he was now ready to take his leave from her sheltering sanctuary. He was ready to climb aboard his ship and focus. His work, his crew, and his ship were waiting for him. He could hear the sea calling, her enticing chant that never failed to lure him out to the open ocean, the place he called home.

Sarah

Nestled amongst the golden straw in Gulliver's stable, Sarah held her best friend's head in her arms. His elderly weakened body was splayed out on the floor. His ungainly position made his painful discomfort clear, and Sarah would not let him suffer.

She nodded solemnly to the vet. It was time. She looked on silently as the vet carefully pushed the sharp needle into Gulliver's soft flesh, and slowly expelled the fatal liquid into his body. Cradling him in her arms, he uttered one last deep throaty nicker, and looking deep into his kind eyes, she watched his gentle soul, her kindred spirit, leave the earthly world they had shared together for twenty-four years. She knew it was the last act of kindness that she could give him. He had told her he was ready; he was weary with age and the pain in his aching joints could no longer be controlled. It was his time. And as much as she didn't want to accept it, she would not let her beloved horse suffer. Her loyal friend, her only friend, he was gone.

"I'm so very sorry, Sarah," whispered Kelly, the yard owner, before she and the vet slowly backed out of the stable to give her some much-needed privacy.

Alone with her tears and thoughts, Sarah cast her mind back to the day Gulliver became hers. She was eighteen, and her whole world revolved around horses. Having finally left school with mediocre A Level results, she had plunged headfirst into fulfilling her dream, to work with horses. She had remained at school to please her uncle, the man who had raised her and loved her as his own daughter. Her mother's brother, James, had taken her in when she was just seven years old after her mother's accidental overdose. Her mother had been dabbling with drugs since her teenage years, and Uncle James had battled with her constantly to try to get her to give them up, especially when Sarah had come along, unplanned. Her mother had tried, she really had, but the monkey on her back would not loosen its grip, and in the end, she could not rid herself from it, and the heart-breaking inevitable had happened.

Sarah didn't really remember her. It was Uncle James who had always looked after her, always taken her in when her mother dumped her on his doorstep, again, because she couldn't manage the responsibility of being a mother. Sarah felt no anger towards her. The drugs had caused her to behave like that. It wasn't who her mother truly was, and for the short periods of time she had managed to remain sober, she had showered Sarah with love and affection. It was something Uncle James had always reiterated. Her mother loved her; the drugs just prevented her from showing her how much.

She had settled into life with Uncle James, and her younger years were happy. She enjoyed his company, and he allowed her to run wild, encouraging her adventures in the woods at the bottom of his garden, and her passion for horses. They had little money; his work became part time the day she officially became his. No niece of his would be walking home from school on her own, nor left alone in the house. He was there for her, always, and what little money he had left over after the bills were paid, he used for riding lessons. And once a year, during her summer holidays, he would take her to Cornwall for a weekend. They would eat ice cream at the beach, and build sandcastles, and splash in the cool, clear ocean waves. And they would picnic on the moors whilst watching the wild ponies graze. Her holidays in Cornwall, with her beloved Uncle James, were some of the happiest memories she had, and she held on to them dearly.

He had promised her, at the age of twelve, that if she finished her education, he would buy her a horse of her very own. Each week, she would show him her completed homework, and in return, he would put some money in a jar. The day she finished her final exam, they cracked open that jar and counted out the result of six long years of saving.

She and Uncle James had discussed many times over the years what kind of horse she would like, but she could never really decide or commit. All she knew was that she would know when she saw him. The search for her best friend began the day she finished her final exam, but it took four months before she found him.

She had arrived home from work, exhausted from a busy day at the local stables, to find her uncle waiting for her. She could tell he had something to share with her as soon as she walked through the door. He was shifting from foot to foot, and unable to settle whilst he dished up her much-needed evening meal. Finally, once she was tucking into the home-made soup, he blurted out that one of his mates from work had mentioned a horse. His sister had purchased him six months ago, but after a while, she had realised they were just not suited for each other, and she was now looking to sell him so she could recoup some money and buy another more suited to her capabilities.

They went to visit him the very next day. The moment she saw him, she knew. And so did her uncle. They both felt it, that indescribable feeling when something is just meant to be. She had unlatched the paddock gate, slipped inside, and watched him. Gulliver had raised his elegant, regal head, and stared right back at her. Slowly, step by step, they had inched towards each other, both drawn by the invisible pull between them, until they were standing directly in front of each other, within touching distance. Sarah's world stopped. She could hear the sound of her own steady breathing, and his. And then he nickered his deep, throaty nicker, just for her. She reached out her hand, slowly and gently, placing it on his velvety soft nose. She could remember that first touch like it was yesterday. It was the moment she was reunited with the other half of her soul.

"Sarah, are you ok in there?" Kelly's voice softly called out over the stable door, bringing her away from her memories, and straight back into the reality of holding her horse's head in her arms. Her horse who was no longer taking breath alongside her.

"It's getting dark," Kelly continued. "You've missed the last bus. Would you like me to take you home?" she asked kindly.

Sarah's mind was spinning with the realisation of what she would have to face when she got home. Her mind and body ached with the knowledge that she would now have to endure life alone, and under the heavy cloud of grief shrouding her. *Without Gulliver, what do I have? What is life without him? How can I carry on? How much longer until he really hurts me? Until he takes it too far and I don't wake up when he knocks me out?* The questions flew around her mind.

Aloud she replied, "He'll kill me."

And to her astonishment, Kelly replied, "I know."

In that moment, both women knew that neither of them were being flippant. Sarah's comment was not the exaggerated remark of a normal wife who had spent too long at the stables. No, she meant it. Julian would literally kill her if he chose to. And somehow, Kelly knew it too.

Sarah felt rooted to the spot. As soon as she left Gulliver, the moment she left the sanctuary of his stable, she would be on her own. Fear enveloped her. She knew what would be waiting for her. And she couldn't get up. She couldn't face him, not today. Her heart was shattered, and her body was weakened by grief.

"I think it would be best if you stay with me tonight," said Kelly, as she unlatched the stable door and joined her on Gulliver's comfy straw bed.

Terror ricocheted through her at the thought of defying Julian. If she didn't go home at all, she knew for sure that blood would be spilled as soon as he laid eyes on her.

As if reading her mind, Kelly continued. "Indefinitely, Sarah. You can stay in my spare room for as long as you need to."

She couldn't speak. It was all too much to take in. Staring blankly ahead of her, she watched Kelly produce a pair of scissors from her coat pocket, and carefully snip a lock of Gulliver's mane. Then she crouched over her, and slipping her strong arms around her, hauled her to her feet.

"It's time to leave him now, he's gone," said Kelly, placing the lock of mane in her hand.

Guided by Kelly, Sarah felt like she was in a trance as she stepped inside Kelly's cosy farmhouse home. And it dawned on her, that over the five years she had stabled Gulliver at her yard, not once had she set foot inside her home. She had been invited, on many occasions, but she could never accept. It was too risky if Julian were to find out, and it was too difficult on her part to make friends with the homelife she had to endure. Over the years Sarah had realised that it was easiest to just keep herself to herself. That way no one would ask questions, and she wouldn't have to fib. Plus, she'd had Gulliver, and he was the only friend she had ever needed.

Kelly's husband, Kyle, was bustling around the kitchen, preparing dinner.

"Sarah's going to stay with us for a while," Kelly announced.

Without missing a beat, Kyle replied, "Welcome, would you like some dinner?"

Sarah stared at the two concerned faces looking back at her, and with a weak smile, she replied, "Thanks, Kyle, but I'm exhausted. I'll just head straight up to bed if that's ok?"

Kyle nodded in reply, and Kelly said, "Of course, I'll take you up." And turning to her husband, she added, "I think it's best you stay in tonight, love. We might get a visitor later."

Sarah saw the knowing look that Kelly and Kyle exchanged and felt shame flooding through her. T*hey know. They know what he does to me, what he's capable of doing to me. How long have they known? Does everyone on the yard know?* She felt her cheeks burn with mortification. She had been so careful, trying to keep her secret. *Clearly not careful enough,* she thought miserably.

Sarah changed into the purple checked cotton pyjamas Kelly had loaned her, pulled back the covers, and climbed into the soft, welcoming bed. Just as she was about to flick out the light, she heard a knock at her door.

"Sarah, can I come in?" Kelly asked.

"Of course," Sarah replied.

Kelly bustled through the door, carrying a tray laden with treats. "I couldn't bear to think of you going hungry," she announced, placing the tray on Sarah's bedside table. "Nothing much, just a little something if you get peckish in the night. Sleep well, Sarah. We can discuss everything in the morning. You're safe now."

"Thank you, Kelly," Sarah stuttered. "Thank you for everything."

"You're most welcome, Sarah. Goodnight," she replied, and then she was gone.

Sarah stared at the tray. There was so much food - a home-made ham salad sandwich, a packet of crisps, a large slice of cake, and two chocolate biscuits, all to be washed down with a steaming cup of tea. Sarah's stomach grumbled. It may well have been the worst of all days, but her eyes had seen the food, and her body wanted it. She took a bite, and another, until she had devoured the whole sandwich. Moving on to the cake, she thought how kind and generous Kelly was. Taking in a virtual stranger, welcoming her into her home, knowing that Julian would cause all kinds of trouble once he found out where she was.

She was too exhausted to think about what tomorrow might bring. After taking the final swig of her tea, she licked the sugar crumbs off her fingers, and for the first time since she could remember, her stomach was content at being full. Snuggling down under the warm duvet cover, she closed her eyes and thought only of Gulliver. With silent tears trickling down her cheeks, she pictured him. She remembered riding him bareback, in a meadow filled with wild flowers, under golden rays of sunshine. She remembered the soft thud of his hooves beneath her, the gentle breeze flowing through her hair, feeling the warmth of his body pressed against hers, and she slowly drifted off to sleep.

Henry

Standing in the middle of the bustling town of Tangier, under the sweltering North African sun, Henry breathed deeply, inhaling the intoxicating scent of Moroccan spices. He liked Morocco. Although the town swarmed with people, the crowds were completely different to the touristy type that mobbed the Canary Islands. Tangier was busy with locals, going about their business amongst the overcrowded market square and numerous higgledy-piggledy alleyways. The stalls were bursting with local produce, each seller hoping to entice a buyer with their stock. Jewellery, clothes, fruits, fabrics, vegetables, spices and livestock - the thriving market had it all, and everything was alive with colour.

Henry weaved his way through the crowds, soaking up the vibrant atmosphere, and made his way towards a narrow, cobbled alleyway. Tangier was a familiar port, and on one of his wanderings, many years ago, he had come across a sweet shop. It was small, squashed in amongst all the other stalls, but every single available space was jam packed with sugary treats. Wine gums were a particular favourite, an indulgence he enjoyed, and he often kept a small stash in his cabin. But nowhere, out of all the ports in the world that he had travelled to, sold wine gums like the ones he found in the off-the-beaten track alleyway in Morocco. Henry smiled to himself, and felt his mouth water as he scanned the haphazardly-stocked shelves and spotted his treasure. He watched the seller open the lid and pour a portion into the white paper bag. And he nodded. Another bag was filled. A second nod, and Henry was happy. Three full bags of sweets should do it.

He popped a red one into his mouth, and blending into the crowd, casually made his way back to the dockyard. His morning off was now over, and it was time to get back to work. Returning to his ship, he smelt the familiar, comforting smell of diesel oil mixed with fresh sea air. He breathed deeply, then stepped on to the gangplank and climbed aboard his ship. No sooner had he set foot on deck, his chief mate scuttled over to meet him. He had clearly been hovering in wait for his return, judging by his unusually flustered demeanour. Waving a piece of paper which he swiftly handed over to him, and with the sound of urgency in his voice, his chief said, "Captain, an urgent message has just arrived for you. You're to call HQ straight away."

Henry nodded his acknowledgment, and after quickly skim-reading his message, he replied, "Thank you, Chief."

Alone in his cabin, Henry digested the information he had just been given. *Unbelievable,* he muttered to himself. *Some people have more money than sense!* Out of the corner of his eye, he caught the chief mate skipping up the stairs to the bridge.

"Chief," he called out. "A quick word, if you please."

Henry took two ice-cold beers out of his fridge, settled himself on his sofa, handed one of the drinks to his chief and indicated for him to take a seat.

"All well, Captain?" asked the Chief.

A tentative smile twitched on his lips; he knew he could be honest with Martin, his chief. They had sailed together for many years. He was loyal, hardworking, trustworthy, and a friend of sorts. They had formed as much of a friendship as was possible between different ranking officers.

"I've been given new orders. The big boss asked for me personally, apparently!" he said with a wry smile. "Apparently my loyalty and dedication to his company has not gone unnoticed. You'll be getting a relief captain from here to South Africa. I'm to join the ship there after a private voyage from Spain to SA for the owner's personal cargo."

The chief's bewildered look did not go unnoticed by Henry. "I know," he continued, "that man has more money than he knows what to do with!"

"And what's the cargo? Did they tell you?" asked Martin, comfortable within the boundaries of their friendship to ask such a question.

And Henry was pleased he did. It could get lonely being at the top. As a leader of men and commander of the ship, it was his responsibility to always remain calm and in control. His responsibility to make the hard decisions, to keep his crew and ship safe at all times. His reliability and leadership skills were critical for running an organised and efficient ship for his men. Although he and the men were there to work, the ship was also their home for many months at a time, and for Henry, it was essential to get the right balance of both work and the crew's much needed down time. But sometimes, it was nice to relax a little, and share his thoughts with someone else. And his chief allowed him to do just that. Neither of them had ever crossed that invisible line between them. And neither of them ever would. They both valued each other as work colleagues, and friends, too much.

"Rich man's toys!" Henry replied. "Fancy cars and posh horses!"

Neither Henry or his Chief had actually met Mr Cooper, the billionaire owner of the shipping company that they worked for, but they had heard many tales of his lavish, playboy lifestyle, and if Henry's memory served him correctly, he had two divorces behind him already. Henry reminded himself, though, that his ships were always kept up to scratch. Mr Cooper believed in high quality vessels for high quality cargo. No rusty old buckets for him to captain, that was for sure. He and the crew were paid handsomely for being a valued part of his international shipping team. And it was well known that for all of his seemingly outrageous ideas and requests, he did in fact work hard for his money, and was always at the forefront of the decision-making for his hugely successful and very profitable business.

"Horses?" exclaimed the chief, breaking into his thoughts. "Real live horses?"

"Yep! For the new wife, apparently. Some sort of special Spanish dancing horses. Four of them. They all look the same to me, but I've been informed that these ones are worth a fortune," admitted Henry. Not knowing anything about horses, Henry was feeling somewhat dubious about carrying four of the things over the open ocean, but he had been told that by sea was how the owner wanted them to be transported, so by sea was how he would have them delivered, no matter what Henry thought of the idea. Orders were orders, and it was not up to him to question them.

And as if the chief could read his thoughts, he said, "Do you have any experience with horses?"

"Nope!" he replied, with a slightly nervous laugh.

"Well," said the chief, "blimey. Did you tell them you don't know anything about horses?"

"I did, and I was told that if I need a horse trainer to accompany me then I should just go ahead and hire one. No expense spared for his wife's passion, apparently. But I didn't get chance to say that my social circle is seriously lacking in horse trainers! Where the hell am I going to find one in a week? Especially one that speaks English. I can't possibly have a guest on a working ship for a month who I can't communicate with."

"Literally more money than sense then!" replied Martin dryly, before continuing. "My brother's wife is into horses. She works with them, I think. She definitely has one of her own. I'll give her a call, maybe she can give you some advice so at least you know a little bit of what you are about to get into!"

Henry gave his friend a grateful smile. "Much appreciated, thank you."

The two men sipped their beers in companionable silence, both taking in the strange turn of events, slightly in awe of how the billionaire lived his extravagant lifestyle. And they were both mulling over the prospect of a captain transporting a group of animals he knew next to nothing about.

After the chief left for his evening duties, Henry slipped off his deck shoes and rested his feet on the now vacated chair opposite him. Rustling the white paper bag containing his treasure, he picked out a yellow one. He closed his eyes and savoured the citrus tang, perfectly blended with a light aromatic spice, and thoroughly enjoyed the sensation as the unique flavours danced amongst his taste buds. He felt the familiar fizz, deep within him, at the prospect of a new adventure ahead of him. Finally coming to terms with the fact he would be in sole charge of such expensive, precious cargo, the novelty of being chosen for such a personal job now lightened his initial foreboding. *I would not have been chosen on a whim*, he mused. *My reputation has preceded me.* Henry felt that after having dedicated his life to his work, his loyalty and commitment were finally being acknowledged. His life at sea always involved some sort of adventure, but this request was one that had even taken him by surprise. He was beginning to look forward to what the month-long voyage might bring, and what tales he would bring back to regale Martin with once they were reunited in South Africa.

Sarah

Sarah was sitting at Kelly's traditional pine wooden kitchen table, her eyes focused on the many weaves and knots that the natural wood had formed before being cut, shaped, and transformed into a beautiful, hand-carved piece of furniture. She had spent two days holed up in Kelly's spare room, crying, grieving, hurting, and panic-stricken as to what Julian would do to her. He knew she was here. She had heard both his and Kyle's raised voices from her room, but Kelly had assured her that everything was fine and that whilst she was cocooned in the farmhouse, she was safe. Now that the much-awaited visit from Julian had happened, the next morning, Kelly had enticed her downstairs with the offer of hot chocolate and pancakes for breakfast.

"I've received some news," said Kelly, and after piling Sarah's plate with pancakes, she filled her own and sat down alongside Sarah.

Before Sarah had a chance to respond, Kelly ploughed on. "Kyle received a phone call from his brother last night. A job opportunity has come up." Kelly placed her hand over Sarah's in a comforting gesture, and added with a gentle smile, "I think it would be perfect for you."

Sarah looked at her new friend. Lovely, kind Kelly, whose eyes were wide and fixed on her, no doubt trying to gauge her thoughts before expanding on the news she had just shared. All Sarah wanted to do was crawl back upstairs, slide into bed, and hide under her duvet. The thought of thinking, planning, decision making – it all overwhelmed her. She felt her skin go clammy. The hole she was in was so big, and so deep, that she couldn't for the life of her fathom a way out of it. She felt her life had become like last year's knotted, twisted up Christmas tree twinkle lights, the type that everyone decided just to throw out because it would be impossible to untangle them.

Except, she thought hopelessly, *I'm not twinkle lights, I can't throw myself out.* Then it dawned on her. Kelly could throw her out. *Oh my word, I've outstayed my welcome.* Mortification swept through her as she tried to read between the lines of what Kelly had just told her. *How could I have been so foolish? How humiliating to have dumped all my problems onto Kelly and Kyle.*

Sarah felt Kelly's hand tighten its grip on her own, and as if reading her thoughts, Kelly said softly, "You're welcome to stay here as long as you like. We're friends, aren't we Sarah?"

Sarah looked up, met Kelly's eyes, and silently nodded.

Seemingly satisfied with her response, Kelly continued. "And friends help each other. Don't think I haven't noticed all the things you have done for me over the years. All the help you have given me with the horses. Every time you leave the yard, every single water bucket is fresh and full, the yard has been swept, tack and rugs that I've just dumped in a hurry have been put back neatly. I know it's you, Sarah, and you have no idea how all those little, thoughtful gestures have helped me out. Now it's my turn to help you."

Sarah felt herself relax under the praise Kelly proffered on her. She wasn't used to being noticed, or having her actions acknowledged or appreciated.

"The stables, your home, it's been my sanctuary," admitted Sarah. "But," she stammered, struggling to hold herself together, "but, without Gulliver, I have no reason to be there anymore."

"You are a gifted horsewoman Sarah," replied Kelly, "and someone with your talent will always be needed. And as far as I can see, you have two options."

Sarah sat up straight, keen to hear what Kelly had to say. It was a relief to know that her friend, unlike herself, could see her situation more clearly, and with her only feasible option to crawl back under someone else's duvet, Kelly's advice might be useful for her.

"Option one," announced Kelly. "You stay with me, and in return for bed and board you can help me with training the horses and general day to day yard work."

Sarah felt relief flooding through her. *She's offering me a job, a job with horses. A chance to get myself back on my feet. An opportunity to live a life independently without Julian.* The thought of Julian made her shudder.

"Option two," continued Kelly, "is the job offer I've just received from my brother-in-law. It would mean leaving here and being far away from Julian. So far away that he would never find you," she said in a quiet, serious voice.

"Where is the job?" she tentatively asked.

"It's only for a month, but the pay is ridiculous! Your bed and board would be included, so your wages could be saved, and it would be enough for a deposit and six months' rent, plus money left over for bills and essentials, giving you plenty of time to get yourself sorted. To make a life for yourself somewhere he can't find you."

Reality was slowly dawning on her. Option one, that would have been her dream job. To stay here, within her comfort zone with her friend, and spend her days surrounded by horses. But Julian would know she was here. She would spend every waking hour terrified that he would find her. That he would sneak up on her when she was alone. It was unrealistic for her to hide behind Kelly and Kyle for the rest of her life. Maybe leaving was her only option? The only way for her to lead a normal life again. But would she ever find the courage to do it? The questions swirled round and round in her head.

Kelly's voice broke through, stilling her mind, and she listened to Kelly explain about the job. "Kyle's brother, Martin, is a chief mate in the Merchant Navy. His captain, and good friend, has been given private orders from the shipping company's owner. He is to transport four Spanish horses from Spain to South Africa. The only problem is, the captain and crew don't know anything about horses, so they're looking for a horse trainer to accompany them for the trip!"

Sarah couldn't believe what she was hearing. Never, in a million years, had she expected to hear about a job being offered to her to travel across the ocean as a horse trainer!

"But I'm not a horse trainer," replied Sarah. As exciting, and terrifying, as the adventurous job opportunity sounded, she was in no way qualified for such a job.

"Of course you are! Everyone on the yard knows how amazing you are with horses, and everyone knows what you've achieved with Gulliver. You probably didn't know, but the other girls would always ask when you were likely to be here, and when you would be schooling Gulliver. They were always keen to catch a glimpse of the two of you 'dancing', as they called it. You and Gulliver were like watching poetry in motion Sarah. I don't think you realise how gifted you are. None of the others can do what you do."

Sarah looked at her, speechless. She had no idea that the other women didn't ride like her. Didn't practice and enjoy classical dressage like she did. It all came so naturally to her, and in all honesty, she just presumed that everyone else in the horse world did everything she did. Learning that she was different was something of a shock.

"Here, let me show you something," said Kelly, whipping out her phone and scrolling through the videos.

She saw Gulliver pop up on her screen and Kelly pressed play. Shostakovich gently flowed out of the speaker, one of her favourite pieces, one she often played when schooling, and she watched herself training Gulliver. She felt pride and heartache build within her as her magnificent horse elegantly and effortlessly performed intricate classical dressage movements in time with the melodic notes. His grey ears were pricked, listening to her subtle cues, his soft hoofbeats gliding across the sand fluidly.

"No one I know rides like this Sarah. I'm sorry if we invaded your privacy by sneaking up and watching you, and filming you," she said with a light laugh, "but in all honesty, we were all completely enthralled by you."

Sarah's heart was thudding in her chest. Her beautiful Gulliver, her entire world, gone.

"Could you send me the video please?" she asked, through broken sobs.

"Of course, I have quite a few actually. I'll send them all to you." After momentarily fiddling on her phone, Kelly continued. "So as you can see, you are more than capable of doing this job, which is what I told my brother-in-law, and the job is yours if you want it."

Just as Sarah was digesting all the information, and potential life changing opportunity, Kyle burst through the door. Noticing them both sitting at the table, he handed over a bag that looked familiar to Sarah.

"I popped over to get some of your things," announced Kyle. "I hope you don't mind. Kelly thought it best I went on my own. She gave me a list." He produced it from his pocket and he turned to his wife. "I got everything on it!" he said proudly.

"Brilliant, thank you. Sit yourself down, I'll make you some pancakes," replied Kelly.

"Thank you so much, Kyle. I was actually dreading having to go back, I really appreciate it," said Sarah.

"No problem at all. Your passport is in there, so you're all good for the job," he said, his concentration now wavering as he watched Kelly serve up a mountain of sugar and lemon pancakes in front of him.

Between mouthfuls of breakfast, Kyle asked, "What are you two girls up to today?"

Sarah had planned to spend yet another day hidden away in bed, but then Kelly said, "I've got two horses to exercise." She turned to Sarah. "I thought we could hack them out together?"

With Kelly's hopeful eyes fixed on her, Sarah felt all she could say was, "Yes, let's go riding."

Sarah was rewarded with a beaming smile from Kelly, and although the effort to drag herself out of the house weighed heavily on her, she knew she must repay the generosity of her friend and muster up a little bit of enthusiasm to help her out with the horses.

Peaches was a lovely little Hafflinger mare who belonged to one of Kelly's full liveries. Kelly looked after her and exercised her during the week, and her adoring owner cared for her and rode her at the weekends. Sarah looked through her little golden ears and settled into the rhythm of her steady walk. Kelly and Jeramiah, another full livery, were ahead of them, leading the way. It felt strange to be riding another horse. For years now, she had only ridden Gulliver, only wanted to ride Gulliver, and she felt the enormity of her loss with each step Peaches took along the familiar route. *If I choose to stay, could I bear the memories? Could I immerse myself in this place without him?* The memories she shared with Gulliver engulfed her. Her throat thickened, her heart ached, and silent tears streamed down her face.

Maybe she did need to get away, she mused, as Kelly led them through the open field and down to the track that would lead them into the woods. Kelly and Jeramiah picked up the pace as soon as they set foot on the woodland track, just like she and Gulliver used to do. Sarah squeezed her legs gently and Peaches swiftly transitioned into a fast canter. With the gentle breeze circling, and the rustling leaves emitting the familiar welcoming sound of the woods, she closed her eyes and let Peaches go. She felt free, and she felt alive for the first time since Gulliver's death. Just being with the horses allowed her to feel again, and through the torturous breaking of her soul, she knew what she had to do.

She opened her eyes when she felt Peaches begin to slow. Ahead of her, Kelly and Jeramiah had reached the end of the track, and Peaches knew it was time to transition back down to her steady walk. As the single file track opened out, she guided Peaches up beside Kelly.

"I'll do it," she said, with a little more determination than she was actually feeling. "I'll take the job." She swept her arm wide, gesturing towards the beautiful countryside. "The memories here, everything reminds me of Gulliver. I think," she continued tentatively, "as much as I would love to take you up on your offer of working for you, I think I need to get away."

Sarah felt Kelly's eyes on her. "I think you're right Sarah, and there's nothing stopping you from coming back here after your month away. The offer for work will still be available to you then. And it was not a completely selfless offer! You would be a serious asset to my business, but I don't think it would be in your best interest right now. Go on the adventure and enjoy being just you. Take this time to learn who you are now that you are not tied down by that awful man."

"Thank you for everything, Kelly," Sarah replied to her friend, and then she felt a little tiny spark ignite within her at what her future might hold.

Henry

Henry climbed aboard the cargo ship that was to be his home for the next month. Agila, that was her name, and although she was a substantially sized vessel, she felt small in comparison to his usual large, commercial container ships. His first task was to climb down into her hold and inspect the living quarters for the horses. He was pleasantly surprised to find four well-constructed stables, each deeply bedded with golden straw and offering its occupant plenty of room for the arduous journey ahead. A large storage area was amply stocked with all the fresh straw and hay they would need, and secure metal bins were filled with what he could only presume was horse feed. At the corner of the feed area, a small area had been turned into a sleeping compartment if the trainer should ever need to stay overnight with her charges down in the hold. All in all, Henry was impressed with the structure and overall consideration that had been given to ensure a safe and secure journey for the horses.

He climbed out of the livestock hold, tracked across the deck of his ship, then stepped down into the second hold. This one was far more like what he was used to. A large open space with four secure areas for the highly prized, ludicrously expensive cars to be stowed away safely until their arrival in South Africa.

Satisfied that all was in order, he made his way to the bridge, and on stepping inside, he was greeted by his new, very enthusiastic chief mate. A ship of Agila's size didn't warrant the same size crew that he was used too, but like everything his shipping owner seemed to do, no money had been spared and he had certainly not been given a skeleton crew. Chief mate, second mate, chief engineer, three able-bodied seamen and a cook. Plus the horse trainer, of course. They would all pull together to make sure that Agila was an efficiently run ship.

"Good morning, Captain," greeted his chief.

"Good morning, Chief," replied Henry.

Henry spent the next two hours familiarising himself with Agila, meeting the rest of his crew, and plotting his course to South Africa. His new chief was proving to be both helpful and extremely knowledgeable in keeping with his rank. Henry had worried that a smaller vessel might have encouraged the shipping owner to hire a less experienced officer than what he was used to, but Henry, in this instance, was happy to have been proven wrong, and felt comfortable that he and the chief were going to get along just fine.

Henry was called away from his duties by his second mate, who announced the arrival of the car which was to take him to the stables. Henry had been informed that his horse trainer, Sarah, had landed safely in Spain, been collected from the airport and was also on her way to the stables. Henry was to meet her there and together, they would meet the horses, and also the head groom of the stables, with whom they would discuss their transportation to the dockyard.

Henry spotted her as soon as his car pulled up outside of the very smart, prestigious Spanish riding school stables. Her pasty white English skin didn't look like it had seen any sun in years, and her wilted shoulders and lacklustre disposition did not make him feel at all confident that she was suitable for the job ahead. Henry sighed deeply to himself, but there was no other alternative available. He climbed out of the car, and filled with his usual calm confidence, strolled over to Sarah and introduced himself.

"Hello Sarah, I'm Captain Henry Hyam. Thank you for being able to get here at such short notice."

Sarah received his offered hand with her own and shook it firmly. With a tentative smile, she met his eyes, and replied, "Hello, Captain."

A slightly awkward pause followed as they both looked around the seemingly empty stables, not knowing what to do next.

"Good flight?" Henry asked, trying to break the tension between them.

"Yes, thank you," she replied politely.

He was struggling to think of a way to keep the conversation going, when Henry was saved by a vibrant man hastily approaching them.

"The Captain, I presume?" he asked, in a thick Spanish accent.

And before Henry had chance to reply, he turned on his heel and marched towards a large barn. "Follow me," he called out.

Raising his eyebrows, he gestured for Sarah to follow. Once inside the barn, Henry realised that this was the area where the horses were trained, and in the middle of the school was a very impressive looking horse.

"This is one of the mares," announced the Spaniard, pointing at the horse. And then he finally acknowledged Sarah's existence. He slowly eyed her up and down, and with a sneer on his face, he drawled, "These horses are not your English cobs."

Henry felt himself stiffen at the obvious and brazen slight towards Sarah. As much as he felt that the petite woman next to him didn't have much presence about her, for the time being, she was one of his crew, and he did not appreciate one of his own being looked down upon. He held himself upright, squared his shoulders, and stepped towards Sarah, a gesture that the Spaniard couldn't miss.

"You must ride the horse," he instructed Sarah brusquely. "You must show me you are capable of looking after such a prized animal. These mares are no peasant English horse."

Bloody hell, he's arrogant, thought Henry, but he noticed that Sarah had not bristled like he had at the Spaniards rudeness. Instead, she looked at him, square in the eyes, and without saying a word, slowly walked over to the horse, which was skittering around on the end of the rope that a young lad was holding on to. He could see the power within the horse as she skipped from hoof to hoof, and as the sunlight shone between the slats of the school's walls, he saw her muscles rippling. At this moment in time, Henry felt grateful that he could stay exactly where he was, at a safe distance from the potential ticking time bomb that was at the end of a very short rope.

He stood back and watched Sarah approach the horse and accept the rope from the young stable hand. Henry thought how small she looked next to the enormous animal, but not once did she cower from the prancing horse. She held her palm out and waited, and as if her quiet calmness filtered through the rope, and seeped into the horse, the mare began to settle, and of its own accord, snuffled Sarah's hand with her nose. Sarah then gently moved her hand and smoothed the mare's face, all the way up, then she positioned herself to begin the same circulation motion across the horse's neck.

Breaking the spell, the Spaniard broke the silence by turning up the classical music that had been playing softly out of the speakers, before yelling, "Now you ride her. Get up."

Henry bristled again at the rudeness of this man, and he also wondered how Sarah was supposed to ride the horse when she didn't have a saddle on?

Once again, it became clear that he had misjudged the capabilities of his horse trainer. In one elegant leap, Sarah was sitting astride the mare. She leaned forward and tied the rope to the other end of the collar that the horse was wearing to improvise as reins, and in her own time, when she was settled, the mare began to walk. Slowly at first, as if Sarah and the mare were introducing themselves to one another, and then it happened. Henry had never witnessed anything like it before in his life. This strange little woman and the big grey horse started dancing. Tiny, delicate steps, perfectly in time with the music, then as the music built into its crescendo, so did Sarah and the horse. The power and speed of the horse was let loose as they effortlessly powered across the sand. Henry watched, transfixed by the dancing duo before him. Guilt surged through him at how he had so wrongfully misjudged this incredibly capable horsewoman. As the music slowed, so did the dancers, returning to the controlled intricate steps, until finally, the music came to an end.

Henry turned to the Spaniard, whose opened mouthed, gawking expression showed him all he needed to know. The smirk had well and truly been wiped off his face, and before the rude little man had the chance to say anything, Henry called out, "Come along now, Sarah. We have paperwork to sort." He met the Spaniard's eye, and in a hard, cold tone, he announced, "Take me to your office."

After the paperwork, travel documents and confirmation for the four horses to be transported to the ship the following day were organised, Henry and Sarah waited outside the stables for their car to arrive. Henry was full of admiration for Sarah and questions about her horsemanship were swimming around in his mind, yet he felt he could not voice them. Once Sarah had left the company of the horses, she immediately fell back into the reserved, almost submissive demeanour that she had greeted him with.

 Henry broke the silence between them. "Are you hungry? Cook should have supper ready for us by the time we get back to the ship." All the while he was thinking that she looked hungry. As well as being petite height wise – she couldn't have been more than five feet four inches - she was also small in frame. Henry thought to use the word slender was being generous, when in fact, she was bordering on skeletal. On closer inspection he noticed her sunken eyes and gaunt features against her pale complexion. Although he noted that her shoulder length mane of golden-brown hair was thick and glossy. And her nature wasn't stand-offish as such, more guarded.

"Ok, thank you," she replied quietly.

She's a conundrum, he thought. He was intrigued to learn more about her and how she managed to get the horse to dance so beautifully. But something told him not to push. Hopefully, when they were out at sea, and when she was down in the hold, in the company of the horses, she might choose to share some of her immense equestrian knowledge with him.

Moments later, their car arrived, and after holding the door open for Sarah to climb in, Henry climbed in beside her. "Back to the ship, please," he instructed the driver.

Sarah

Encased in the back of the air-conditioned car, Sarah closed her eyes and rested her head against the window. She felt like she was on a carousel. Round and round she went, but the ride never seemed to stop. She was grateful that the captain was quiet alongside her, seemingly lost in his own thoughts, just as she was, whilst listening to the softly flowing Spanish music from the car radio.

Persephone, that was the horse's name that she had been asked to ride. She had been on auto pilot, and with her merry-go-round mind whizzing in every direction, she had been grateful to have been given something to focus on. As soon as she had taken hold of Persephone's lead rope, her mind had steadied, and she had been able to live right in the moment. The grey mare accepted her quickly, and when she heard the music strike up, her body took over. The subtle cues she used to give Gulliver worked equally well on the astonishingly well-trained Persephone, and together, as one, they had danced. For those few moments in time, she was lost in a world of just her and the horse. Not knowing the horse's capabilities, Sarah had not asked for too much too soon, but after Persephone executed her half pass in trot exceptionally on both reins, her flying changes seemed effortless, and Sarah realised her capabilities. Accepting Sarah's cue, and in perfect time to the music, with perfect rhythm and impulsion, Persephone executed the piaffe. Her grey ears were pricked, and she was steady and calm, listening to her rider. She was waiting, and Sarah knew just what she was waiting for, and when Persephone gave her the cue that she was ready, Sarah asked. With the sound of the classical crescendo building, the magnificent horse beneath her effortlessly performed a perfect levade before Sarah let her free to stretch out her muscles and canter on a loose rein around the school.

And then it was all over, and her aching soul and grief-ridden heart took her over once again. She missed Gulliver with every fibre of her body, and to have ridden Persephone so effortlessly, so wonderfully, just like she did Gulliver, brought her tragic loss to the forefront of her very being. She bit her lip, trying desperately to slow the imminent outpour of tears that were swelling within her. *I must remain professional,* she told herself, inwardly fretting that her silence and lack of conversation were not in the least bit professional.

"We're here," announced the captain.

Sarah watched the driver hand over the paperwork to the officials at the dock yard gates. The barrier went up, and the car slowly weaved its way through the busy dockyard. Men were purposefully going about their business and heavy machinery was in full swing as the merchant ships' cargo was unloaded and loaded, ready for the next voyage. Sarah had never seen anything like it before. Her little world of English woodland tracks, pretty meadows, and her beloved Gulliver seemed a million miles away. *A different life.*

Stepping out of the air-conditioned car, the sweltering Mediterranean heat hit her. She took it all in – the strong smell of diesel oil, and the taste of the salty tang of the warm sea air. Despite all her misery, she couldn't help but feel that it tasted like freedom. And that thought was just enough to quell her burgeoning tears, as she looked up and took in the enormous ship before her.

"Welcome to Agila," Henry said, with a grin on his face. "She's only small, but we have everything we need for the voyage and for the horses to be safe and comfortable for the journey."

"Small?" squeaked Sarah, in disbelief. "It's huge."

"She," said the captain. "All ships are referred to as she."

Sarah felt her face flush at her ignorance, and as if sensing her unease, the captain continued. "She's a small cargo ship, perfect for what we need, and her size means we can travel slightly faster than we could on the larger merchant vessels the company owns. The owner thought speed was the key for the horses," he said kindly to her. "Plus," he continued with a wry laugh, "he wants the horses as soon as possible for his new wife!"

Sarah smiled in return, keen to explore her new home for the next month.

"Shall we climb aboard?" asked Henry, pointing to the gangplank.

After acknowledging her nod, Henry picked up her small case and said, "Follow me."

Sarah quietly followed the captain to board Agila. Once she set foot on the deck, he pointed out the two holds, one for the horses and one for the cars, then turning on his heel, he marched towards the ship's accommodation. She skipped up the four flights of steps behind him until he stopped outside a door.

"The owner's cabin," he announced. "This will be yours whilst you are with us. Mine is next door, come and find me once you've got settled." And with a warm smile he handed over her bag, stepped away, and into his own accommodation.

Sarah hadn't actually thought about where she would be staying. Everything had happened so fast, and with her overwhelming emotions swallowing her up, her only focus had been to escape Julian's toxic clutches, and block out, as best she could, the raw pain and all-consuming devastation of losing Gulliver. And somehow, she seemed to have woken up from her daze and found herself on a Merchant Navy ship. She clicked open the door and stepped inside. It was more spacious than she had expected. Ahead of her was a seating area and table, and she noticed the well-stocked bookshelves too. To the side was a fridge. She pulled open the door to find it stocked with soft drinks, light beers and a selection of chocolate bars. She opened the door to her right to find an ample sized cabin bed, immaculately made up, and a built-in cabinet for her clothes. Another door brought her into her own ensuite shower and toilet room. Everything was perfectly pristine with fresh, white fluffy towels and selection of toiletries for her.

After unpacking, Sarah took a quick shower to freshen up, changed into clean clothes and looked at herself in the bathroom mirror. *You've got a job to do. You need the money. You desperately need the money. It's time to start making a good* impression to the captain. And with a determined nod, she stepped outside of her cabin and tentatively knocked on Henry's open door.

She heard footsteps behind her. "Come on up," said Henry, before he turned around and went back up the stairs he had appeared from.

Sarah did as she was told and climbed the stairs ahead of her. She stepped into what she could only presume was the control room. Computer devices, screens, buttons. So *many buttons! I wonder what they could all possibly do!* Navigation equipment and charts were laid out. *This is where it all happens,* thought Sarah, soaking up the whole new world she had stepped into. And the view! She could see right over the bustling dock yard, out across to the other end of the ship, and far out to sea.

"The bridge," Henry announced. "Come on in." He gestured for her to stop hovering in the doorway and join him properly on the bridge.

"Settled in ok?" enquired Henry.

"Yes, thank you," she replied, acknowledging how polite and thoughtful the captain was towards her.

"Good," he replied, his warm smile making her feel welcome on his ship. "It's supper time, I'll take you down and introduce you to the crew."

After her introductions to the crew had been made, Sarah enjoyed the simple but delicious meal of rice, chicken, and Mediterranean vegetables in the officers' mess with the captain, chief mate and second mate. Both were as equally friendly and polite as Henry. The captain informed them all that they were to be on deck at six am sharp, ready for the cars and horses to arrive. They were to set sail as soon as everything was safely onboard the ship.

Sarah parted from the officers, stating that she was exhausted from her long day. She couldn't quite believe that it had started in England! She climbed the four flights of stairs alone, looking forward to the sanctuary of her quiet cabin. Settling herself in bed, she sent a quick message to Kelly, informing her that all was well and the horses, the captain and the ship were all amazing. And then she couldn't help herself - she clicked open on the video Kelly had sent her last week. Shostakovich flowed out of the speaker and Gulliver appeared before her. Her heart swelled, her throat burned, her skin prickled under the grief ridden heat, and the tears poured out of her. Over and over again she watched her beautiful friend elegantly dance to the music.

The sharp shrill bleeps of her phone alarm startled her and drew her from her slumber at quarter past five the next morning. She woke with her phone still in her hand and it took her a moment to remember where she was, as the unfamiliar surroundings slowly became familiar again. She jumped out of bed, eager for the distraction from her burden of bereavement, and keen to show the captain that she was both reliable and professional.

Just as she placed her hand on the door handle, she heard a loud knock on her door, on opening it, she came face to face with the captain.

"Good morning," she greeted him.

"Good morning, it's time to go. The horses are here," replied Henry.

Though early, the Spanish sun welcomed her with warmth when she stepped out on deck amongst the hubbub of activity. She watched the four Aston Martin cars - one racing green, one navy blue, one blood red and one a sparkling silver – as they were loaded and secured into the hold.

"You're up now, Sarah," called out the chief mate, as the crane carefully lifted up the large crate that the horses had been placed in to lower them down into the hold.

She followed the chief mate along the deck then down into the horses' hold. She could sense the horses' stress and anxiety as soon as she approached the crate.

She confidently asked all of the men to leave, announcing that the horses would settle much more quickly in a calm, quiet environment.

She slid back the latch, opened the door a crack, and peeped inside the crate. Four horses, eyes wild with fear and their muscular bodies dripping in sweat, stared back at her.

"Hi there, girls," she said softly, then stepped back, opened the door and allowed them to step into the hold. They were nervous. The strange smells emanating from the ship and the loud noises from the heavy machinery working on the dockyard unsettled them. It was all a far cry from the calm, tranquil horse yard that they used to call home. Demeter, the matriarch of the herd, stepped out first, taking her time to acknowledge her new surroundings. She was closely followed by the other three mares jostling behind her. Sarah waited patiently for them all to leave the crate in their own time. The four loose stalls were large and airy, large enough for Sarah to make the decision to stable them in their natural pairs to begin with. She thought being close might help them to adjust for the arduous journey ahead. She guided Demeter and her daughter Persephone into one, and whilst they cautiously investigated their new lodgings, she bolted the lock to secure them inside. Diana and Artemis, paternal sisters, she carefully herded into the other. Relief flooded through her once all four horses were calmly settled in their respective stables.

Sarah had requested that all their feed and hay came from the Spanish horse yard. It was imperative that they had as little change as possible during their journey. The last thing she needed was a colicking horse out in the middle of the ocean. Once the horses were fed and given their slice of hay, and she had double-checked their buckets of water were full, she whispered, "I'll be back soon," then took her leave from her charges. The captain had reiterated to her again that morning how important it was that their strict time schedule was adhered to. They were to leave as soon as she gave the word that the horses were safely secured in their stables.

Sarah climbed out of the hold, briskly marched across the deck, then skipped up the flights of stairs to the bridge. Henry was waiting for her, his expression telling her that he was keen to get going, and before he had chance to ask, she blurted out, "Everyone is safe and secure," and followed it up with a broad smile.

"Excellent, thank you Sarah," he replied. Then indicating to a man that she had not seen before, he announced, "This is our pilot, he'll be guiding us out of the port and into the shipping channel."

"Hello," said Sarah to the pilot, then she anxiously hovered in the doorway, not knowing what she was expected to do.

Acknowledging her discomfort, Henry said, "Take a seat," pointing to one of the control chairs. The deep rumble of the ship signalled that the engines had started, and she quietly sat down whilst the men got to work. She kept her hands on her lap, fearful that she might accidentally press one of the many intimidating buttons in front of her. Whilst enjoying the spectacular view that the bridge offered her, she listened to them talking. *Shipping talk? Navy talk? Navigation talk?* She felt somewhat ignorant that she had no idea of any naval terminology at all, but all the while she found herself enjoying being part of the busy goings on of a real-life commercial ship.

She was still glued to her seat half an hour later, when the pilot came over to her and said his goodbyes. His small pilot boat had arrived to take him back to shore, his work now done. Sarah cast her eyes back out to sea and pondered what it would be like when they were in the middle of the ocean with no sign of land for days and days. The idea of such solitude, on board this little ship, out there amongst the natural elements, with the horses, sent a little thrill through her body. Her adventure was about to begin.

Henry

Henry sipped his black coffee. It was three o'clock in the morning and he was on night watch, staring out into the black abyss of the open ocean from his bridge. He liked being alone on the bridge at night. He found it immensely peaceful, and he welcomed the solitude after the previous hectic few days of organising the horses. He had felt somewhat out of his depth when it came to the flighty animals, but here, at the helm of his ship, in the silence of the night, he finally felt a sense of calm returning to him. He was back where he belonged, in charge of his ship, far out at sea.

Relaxing in his comfy leather control chair, he allowed his mind to wander to Sarah. His reserved, steady nature and many years of experience enabled him to trust his intuition and confidently lead his men. Over the years, he had capably learnt to read people. He had to - it was his job to keep everyone on board his ship safe. And he always knew when there was a bad apple amongst his crew. He relied on his instincts when it came to his men and working out who he could trust and depend on, and who he could not. That was almost more important.

But when it came to Sarah, there was just something about her that muddled his mind. There was something about her that he just couldn't put his finger on. She seemed pleasant enough. She was polite to both him and the crew, and she diligently went about her work with the horses. Truth be told, you wouldn't even know she was there because she was so quiet and unintimidating. But, there was something. She has a sort of sadness about her. In some ways he was grateful she was so timid and unintrusive. He had worried that having a woman on board might distract his men, especially if she was the vivacious sort. Not that he had anything against women like that. Quite the opposite, in fact - he found their company very enjoyable indeed, but not when he was at work. And Sarah was most definitely not a distraction. He barely saw her. Occasionally he bumped into her. He was fairly certain she liked classical music because he heard it playing quietly from her cabin, and she had shared with him how much she enjoyed having her own mini library, so he had assumed that when she was not at work, or in the officers' mess, she was in her cabin reading.

His thoughts were disturbed when his chief mate relieved him from duty at six o'clock. He slipped into his cabin for a quick shower and shave, then eagerly made his way down to the officers' mess, his mouth watering at the thought of the cooked breakfast waiting for him.

He made small talk with the cook, and after complimenting him on his delicious breakfast, the cook surprised him by saying, "I hope you don't mind, Captain. I was hoping to make a slight change to dinner this evening. Sarah showed me how to make a treacle sponge pudding yesterday and I'm eager to give it a go and make it for you all today. Would that be ok?"

"Of course, I look forward to trying it," replied Henry. Intrigued to know how Sarah and the cook ended up cooking together, he carefully continued, "That was kind of Sarah to show you."

"Oh yes," enthused the cook. "She didn't come in for lunch yesterday because she was so busy with the horses. I waited, but after I had finished clearing up after lunch and she still hadn't turned up, I decided to take lunch to her. She needs feeding up, don't you think?"

Henry did indeed agree that Sarah was in need of the cook's hearty meals, but before he had chance to reply, the cook ploughed on. "So I wrapped her up a sandwich and took it down to the stables. She was so grateful. I think it's hard work for her clearing out all of the muck. Anyway, we got chatting about food and she told me her favourite was treacle sponge pudding. Once she found out I didn't know how to make it, well, to repay me for bringing her lunch to her, when she finished work, she came straight to the kitchen and showed me!" The cook finished with a grin, full of enthusiasm for their newest crew member.

Henry was privately pleased to hear that his cook had been looking after Sarah. While she appeared content with only the horses for company, it was nice to know that the cook had been a little bit of company for her, if only for a short time. They had been at sea for just over a week now and other than polite conversation when they bumped into each other, they'd both been kept busy with their own duties, and now he decided that he really should have a proper catch up with his horse trainer. Taking his leave from the cook, he strolled across the deck then climbed down into the horses' hold.

Sarah was inside one of the stalls, sandwiched between two horses with a grooming brush in her hand. He could see her talking to them softly. The sound of the engines prevented him from hearing what she was saying, but the way the horses twitched their ears at her gave the impression that they were deep in conversation. He watched one of the horses nudge Sarah gently with her nose, seeking her attention and reminding her that she wanted to be groomed too. Sarah's face broke out into a beaming smile as the horse showed her impatience by giving her another nudge.

Henry noticed how happy and relaxed she looked, squished in amongst the horses. Sarah had explained how pleased she was with the generous size of the stalls, but for Henry, seeing them filled with two large horses made him feel positively claustrophobic at the thought of standing in there with them.

Sarah was totally engrossed with her charges, her quiet voice whispering away to them, and from the way the horses' ears twitched this way and that, Henry had the strangest feeling that the horses could understand every word she said. In her company, the horses were calm and relaxed, and focused only on her. Henry walked right up to the stalls, and with her back towards him, totally immersed in what she was doing, Sarah had still not noticed him.

He was barely three feet away from her when he thought he should probably announce his presence. He called her name, and without meaning too, his voice came out far louder than he intended, and he saw Sarah freeze.

"Sarah," he said, much more quietly the second time. And as she turned to face him, he saw a look of sheer terror in her eyes. A look that startled him so much he actually turned around to see what might have frightened her, but as he looked around to the empty space behind him, it dawned on him that it was him that had caused such fear in her eyes. By the time he looked back at her, the wild-eyed look had vanished, as quickly as it came, and Sarah had composed herself.

"You scared me!" she said to him. Her tone was light, but it was clear that her feelings were much more intense. Her reaction did not seem usual for someone who had been startled by accident. Neither she nor the horses moved from their positions, and she remained sandwiched between them. And that was when Henry felt his intuition kick in, that somehow these horses knew something that he didn't know. At this moment in time, it wasn't Sarah who was keeping the horses calm, it was them who were instinctively protecting one of their own, because she was frightened. And for reasons known only to them, it was him that they were protecting her from.

"I'm sorry, Sarah, I didn't mean to startle you."

Sarah waved his apology away with her hand. "Don't worry about it, I wasn't expecting you, that's all," she replied, yet stayed firmly rooted to the spot, making no attempt to remove herself from in between the mares.

He was flummoxed as to what to say next. He cleared his throat. "When you've finished with the horses could you pop up to my cabin so I can have update on them please?"

"Yes, of course," she replied, and Henry could see the relief flood through her on realising that he would now leave, and she would be left alone in the company of just the horses.

"Until later then," was all Henry felt he could say before turning on his heel and swiftly walking away.

Climbing back up onto the deck, he decided to head over to the bow of his ship. He looked out to the sprawling Atlantic Ocean before him and watched the bright rays of sunshine glisten across the undulating surface, all the while enjoying the warmth from the breeze, coupled with the cool, salty, sea spray splashing against his skin. *She's a mystery,* he thought, *and what secrets do those horses know that I don't?*

As Henry idly stared off into the distance, he realised how little he knew about the woman living in the cabin next door to his. There had been no formal interview for the job, and he had certainly not requested or seen any proof of her qualifications. It had all happened so quickly, and he had put his trust in his fellow officer and friend, who in turn had put his trust in his sister in law's choice for the horse trainer he now had on board his ship. But the horses were being well cared for, and she was certainly an excellent horse woman, so on reflection, that really was all he needed to know. The mystery that was her past, and her reasons for accepting the somewhat unusual job transporting horses halfway across the world by merchant ship, were not really any of his business at all.

Sarah

Sarah was settled in her makeshift cabin bed alongside the horses' stables trying to focus on *Anne of Green Gables*. It was one of her favourite books and she had been delighted to find it on the shelf in her cabin. She was desperately trying to escape into the world of the plucky red-headed orphan and idyllic setting of Prince Edward Island, but she had read the same page three times, and nothing was going in.

It had been three days since the awkward, humiliating moment when Henry surprised her in the stables. She was utterly mortified at her own reaction to such a perfectly innocent greeting. She wasn't afraid of Henry, and she felt perfectly safe being far out at sea with only men for company. It was Julian who frightened her, no one else, and deep down she knew that Henry wasn't going to hurt her. It was the shadow that had fallen over her and the sound of his breathing that took her right back into the eye of the storm. It wasn't Henry's fault that he had unintentionally approached her just like Julian used to do, before the familiar wallop was delivered, knocking the wind out of her, and sending her flying to the floor before the real torment and abuse started. When she felt his shadow fall on her she had frozen on instinct, her body physically and mentally preparing itself for the blow that was to come. She tried to remind herself that after suffering such abuse for so many years, it would take a long time for those protective instincts to dissipate. She had been so grateful to have been standing between Demeter and Persephone. Hiding behind them had given her chance to regain control of her unwitting reflex reaction before composing herself and responding to Henry. She had hoped desperately that he had not noticed, but deep down she knew that he had. His immediate departure from the stables told him that he had, along with the slightly puzzled expression on his face.

She had gone to see him an hour later to discuss the horses, just as he had asked her to do. She had put on her brightest smile and in a somewhat hurried manner, whittered on about the horses and assured him that everything was fine, before explaining she still had chores to do. Then she left as quickly as she had arrived, leaving Henry with yet another baffled look on his face.

Sarah sighed, closed her book, and rolled off the bed. She decided to do something productive, because reading wasn't taking her mind off anything. Picking up the grooming box, she slipped into the sisters' stable. "Hello girls," she said softly, then pulled out a brush and gently groomed Diana's mane. All four of the grey mares reminded her of Gulliver. During the time they had been in her care, she was beginning to learn their own little individual quirks, but they had the same gentle temperaments and similar beautiful grey coat that her Gulliver had. It was mixed blessings for all four horses to be so like her own beloved Gulliver. The ache for him was always at the forefront of her mind, the pain of the colossal loss of her dearest friend, but she also enjoyed remembering his little quirks, those things that made him an individual, and the things that made her love him more than any other living being.

She felt a darkness shroud her when she recalled how Julian had tried to sell him. He knew Gulliver was worth a fortune after all the extensive training she had done with him, and Julian didn't like her to have anything of her own, or anything that he could not control. She remembered the argument they had, and the state she had been in the next morning, but no matter how hard he beat her, she would not give him up. And she remembered how Julian had then used Gulliver to his own advantage. Usually, Sarah kept herself to herself after the beatings to give herself time to recover and for the bruises to fade. But one particular time, a work colleague of Julian's popped over unannounced the next evening, and had seen the state that Sarah was in. Bowled over with shock at the sight of her, he had quickly asked if she was alright and how on earth had she ended up in such a state. And as quick as lightning Julian had informed him that she had fallen off her horse, followed by a hearty laugh, jesting that everyone knew what horsey women were like! And the work colleague had accepted the tale on the spot. And so Julian had used Gulliver as his excuse, each and every time anyone saw Sarah covered in bruises.

Sarah bit back the tears of the unfairness of it all. Not once, during all the years she and Gulliver shared together, had he ever hurt her, and nor had she ever fallen from him. Her beautiful, gentle, loyal friend had been blamed repeatedly for something he didn't do, and would never have done to her. And she thought back to what he had given her. Solace and love during the entirety of her toxic marriage. A loyal and unwavering friendship, and the only reason she had to get up and face each day. He was her one constant amongst her husband's unpredictable, viscous bouts of temper and cruelty. Her tears spilled freely as she realised and finally understood the final gift her dearest friend had given her. Freedom. Even in death he had stayed loyal and true to her, and with his passing he had enabled her to finally escape Julian's clutches. He had given her the strength to be brave, and after all the wonderful things she had achieved with him, the partnership he had willingly and eagerly shared with her, she was now able to use her knowledge and skills to take her far away from Julian.

A moment of gratitude swept through her when Diana nickered a deep, intimate nicker, whilst nuzzling her with her nose. It was thanks to Gulliver that she was here, right now, in the company of four magnificent horses, and Sarah wrapped her arms around the sweet-tempered mare and buried her face in her mane. As she stood, embracing the horse, allowing herself to enjoy the heartfelt moment with Diana, she felt the ground beneath her roll. Methodically at first, almost as if the sea was trying to lull her sleep, but with each passing moment, the force behind the rocking quickened and Sarah was beginning to lose her balance. Holding on to Diana, she edged her way to the stable door and carefully slipped outside before securely bolting the latch.

She clung to the edge of the stables and slowly eased her way towards the feed store. She would have to let go in order to take the two steps necessary to reach the entrance before grabbing hold of the rail inside, then she could inch her way to the security of the bed. With each lurching movement of the ship beneath her, she felt her insides swell and nausea rise within her. She focused on trying to maintain her balance, trying to pre-empt the rise and fall of the tumultuous waves, before releasing her hands from the stable. A violent surge threw her off her unsteady feet, her head hitting the heavy steel floor. She gasped and winced as the sharp pain swept through her. Pulling herself up onto her hands and knees, she inelegantly crawled her way to the sanctuary of the bed. She heaved herself up, and lying flat in her back, with blood trickling down her cheek, she gripped the firm wooden sides of the bed, knowing that she could not move again until the raging sea had calmed.

Sea sickness had been one of her concerns when deciding to take the job. She had never travelled any great distance by boat before, let alone lived on board a working naval ship for a month. However, once the engines had started, and the ship had powered through the waves, out into the open ocean, her fears had calmed. It had not taken her long to adjust to the gentle rocking motion of the ship. In fact, she actually rather liked it, and she had secretly felt pleased that she suffered no signs of sea sickness whatsoever. Sarah now realised how easily she had been lulled into a false sense of security by the enchantress of the deep. The nausea ebbed and flowed throughout her body with every swell and sway, with bile rising in her throat, and for the first time since boarding the ship, she felt fear. The ship had looked so humongous to her, so solid and strong, and she seemed to have held an air of pride whilst docked alongside the Spanish port. Now, the ship seemed tiny, like a baby bunny facing a ferocious lion, and so very inconsequential against the aggressive storm raging all around her.

She glanced towards the horses, and much to her surprise she noticed very little change in their behaviour. They were standing square, bracing themselves against the rolling waves, their ears pricked, alert to the new motion of their stables, but still contentedly munching on their hay.

"Sarah."

She heard her name being called loudly above the sound of the engines.

"Sarah, are you there?"

And she looked up to see the captain standing in the entrance of the feed store.

"Sarah, are you ok?" asked Henry, concern etched on his face. "Oh my god, you're hurt," he blurted out.

Sarah watched him shift uncomfortably in the doorway, as if he was undecided about what to do next.

"I slipped and fell," she replied. "I'm ok," she said, trying to reassure him.

He looked at her, and she felt his eyes darting between her own and the cut on her head.

"Can I," he stuttered, "can I come in?"

She nodded; it was all she could manage when another wave of nausea engulfed her. She watched him pick up the tea towel she used for drying out the horses feed buckets and tentatively sit down on the side of the bed. Raising the tea towel in his hand, he looked at her, and after acknowledging her second nod, her slowly pressed it against her head. She winced at the touch, but the towel was still damp and offered a cooling sensation against the burning pain.

"I thought I had better come down and check on you with the storm," said Henry. "Down here is the best place for you to be," he continued, still carefully tending to her gash. "The closer you are to the keel, the less fierce the waves are."

He looked at her and smiled. "It doesn't look too bad, it should heal in no time." He eased himself away from her, somewhat embarrassed, she thought, at their close proximity, and settled himself at the bottom of the bed. He stood, briefly, before moving something that was underneath the crumpled blanket. "Ah, *Anne of Green Gables*," he announced, "one of my favourites!"

Another swirl of nausea caused her to bring her hand up to her mouth, the fear of actually being sick rising within her. After a brief moment, the feeling passed and her dignity was left intact, at least for the moment.

"Seasick?" he asked her kindly.

"I'm afraid so," she admitted.

"It's best not to think about it, try and focus on something else." He waved the book at her. "Let me see where you're up too. Chapter six, that's a good one!" he said, with a twinkle in his eyes.

Sarah watched him smooth out the page in front of him. He tentatively cleared his throat, and then he began to read. She focused on his steady voice and cast her mind to the fictional world of the little red-headed orphan and the enchanting setting of Prince Edward Island.

Henry

Henry was standing on the bridge, sipping his morning coffee, enjoying the view of clear skies and a calm sea before him. His eyes were drawn to the ship's deck when he noticed a somewhat dishevelled Sarah emerging from the horses' hold. He watched her stroll across the deck before slipping inside to head into the ship's quarters, and out of his line of sight. He thought how well she looked, sea sickness aside, in comparison to the first day he had met her three weeks ago. Her pale skin now sported a golden sun-kissed tan, and with the amount of food the cook kept feeding her, it was no surprise that she had lost the appearance of a gaunt skeleton and now had a much healthier glow about her. He was beginning to find her more and more attractive as the days went by.

He had very much enjoyed reading to her the previous night. It had been a long time since he had read *Anne of Green Gables*; it had been a favourite of his mother's and he had fond memories of her reading it to him when he was a little boy. A wave of sympathy had swept over him when he had found Sarah, gripping the makeshift bed rail tightly with a glimmer of fear in her eyes. For him, the storm had been nothing. It was just the usual, as far as a life at sea went, and certainly nothing to be concerned about in comparison to some of the horrendous weather conditions he had endured over the years. But it had dawned on him, as soon as he saw her, that all of this was unknown to her and very much outside of her comfort zone. He hoped that she found his kindness genuine, and that it showed her how much he valued her presence on his ship. That he appreciated having such a knowledgeable woman in charge of the horses. She was very much a valued member of his crew, and he always took great care of his men - or women, of course - putting their needs before his own. He had sensed a vulnerability in her last night, and he hoped, that by supporting her in her time of need, that she would begin to trust him and open up about her reasons for accepting such a job, and possibly share a little about herself. He found her most curious, and unlike any other woman he had ever met. And he had to admit it to himself, he found her very intriguing indeed, and not only in a professional capacity.

"Good morning, Captain," said Sarah.

Her presence on the bridge, standing right in front of him, pulled him away from his daydreaming. He felt a brief rush of colour flush to his cheeks, suddenly alert that his musings were not completely professional, before hastily composing himself, and replied, "Good morning, Sarah." And he gestured for her to take a seat in the control chair next to him.

She was now in fresh clean clothes, her hair still damp from her morning shower, and a subtle hint of citrus wafted over him as she walked past him, a scent he found himself liking very much.

"Thank you so much for looking after me yesterday," she blurted out in an almost embarrassed tone, looking slightly abashed. "I'm clearly not much good to anyone, especially the horses, when a storm comes along!"

He watched her slowly look up and meet his eye. He smiled at her, and in what he hoped was a warm, friendly tone, he replied, "No need to apologise Sarah, we all know what it's like to be caught off guard in a storm. I slipped and got thrown down a flight of stairs once when I was a cadet! Luckily our second mate found me and hauled me too my feet, dragged me into the nearest cabin and strapped me in the bed so I couldn't do any more damage to myself during the storm!"

He watched her relax as he shared his own misfortune with her. Her softened body posture encouraged him to continue, and, hoping that she would share something about herself with him in return, he said, "As with everything in life, experience is the key. No doubt you could teach me a thing or two about horses! I know absolutely nothing about them, and I certainly didn't know that they could dance. The way you rode Persephone in Spain, well, I've never seen anything like it. Have you always liked horses?"

He watched her cheeks colour under his praise, and he waited quietly for her to reply. After a momentary pause, she spoke.

"Ever since my Uncle James took me for my first riding lesson when I was a child. The moment I set foot on that horse yard, I just felt like it was where I was supposed to be, somewhere I belonged."

Her bright blue eyes looked up at him, and she continued, "No doubt it was the same feeling you had when you first climbed aboard a ship!"

"Indeed!" he replied heartily, "I know exactly what you mean."

Feeling that the conversation was going well, and noting to himself that he was somewhat reluctant for it to end just yet, he took a chance, hoping that he was not pushing her too much too soon, and said, "Do you have your own horse at home in England?"

Her posture changed in an instant. The rigid, self-protective stance that he knew so well was back. He felt his own heart sink, knowing he had somehow floundered into her private territory again. Admonishing his mistake, he instantly replied, "My apologies, Sarah, I did not intend to intrude on your private life."

The air was silent between them; however, she did not get up and leave. He looked away from her, far out to sea, and waited to see how the situation would unfold. He did not know how long they were silent for, he focused only on not looking at her, desperately trying to imply that no pressure was upon her, and that she was most definitely free to get up and leave if that is what she wanted to do.

Eventually, he heard her quiet voice break the silence. "His name was Gulliver. My Uncle James bought him for me when I was eighteen."

Henry noticed a wistful look glaze over her eyes, before he replied, "It sounds like you have a very lovely uncle."

She nodded in reply, seemingly lost in her own world for a few brief seconds, and then to his delight, she continued.

"Yes, I was very lucky with my Uncle James. He actually raised me."

Henry knew better than to ask why she had been raised by her uncle, and not her parents. He sensed that it was not the way she was intending the conversation to go. Instead, he nodded, indicating that he was keenly listening to her story.

"I lost him shortly after I got Gulliver, but I was so very grateful that he had been there with me when we found him. He had a chance to get to know the horse we had talked about getting me for years. And I know that he knew how wonderful Gulliver was, how perfect he was."

She cast her eyes out to the open ocean and the seconds slipped by between them. Again, Henry knew that he should not interrupt, or offer any response regarding the loss of her uncle. He knew she was not seeking comfort or pity; she was merely stating a fact.

"Would you like to see him?" And after acknowledging his raised brow, she said, "Gulliver, I mean. Would you like to see Gulliver?"

Curiosity had been circulating through him ever since their tentative conversation had begun. He mentally steadied his voice, so as not to appear too eager, before saying, "Yes, very much."

He was rewarded with her warm smile, and then she dug her phone out of her pocket, fiddled with the buttons, and passed it over to him.

"It's a video," she stated, "just press the play button."

Taking her phone in his hands, he pressed the button and Shostakovich softly filled the quiet bridge. The same music he had heard playing from her room nearly every evening since she had come aboard his ship. The video sprang into life; a magnificent horse being ridden by Sarah without a saddle or bridle, and they were dancing. He had thought she was wonderful with Persephone, but seeing her on Gulliver, he could see that her horse was in a class of his own. Each and every step was perfectly in time with the music. Sarah and Gulliver seemed to be floating on air. He watched in awe. It was a partnership of two equals, with both parties focused and dedicated to perfecting their unique art. Both lost in their own world, a world where he felt only Sarah and Gulliver existed. Once the music ended, he watched Sarah and Gulliver come to a halt in the middle of the sand school. Sarah leant forward and wrapped her arms around the horse, as if praising him for his work. She elegantly slipped off him and moved to stand directly in front of him. He watched her rest her forehead against his, and together they stood in their secret, private world.

Henry felt his throat thicken. Watching the intimate scene unfold before him, he almost felt like he was intruding, but he could not look away. He could not take his eyes off the regal horse and his beautiful mistress. Henry knew he had never felt a connection with any other living being like the one he was witnessing through the screen. And he noted privately, *if I can feel emotion just from watching a video, what must it be like to feel like that in real life? What must it have felt like for Sarah and Gulliver?* And in that moment, for the first time in his life, Henry felt a sensation that he could only assume was envy.

Sarah held out her hand, indicating that his video show, his glimpse into her world, was over. Reluctantly returning her phone, in a voice laden with emotion that he could not hide, and did not want to hide, he said, "Gulliver is a truly magnificent horse."

"Yes," she agreed politely. "Yes he was." And fiddling with her phone so as not to look at him, she finished with, "He passed away last month."

"I'm so very sorry, Sarah," was all he could say. What could he say to someone who had so evidently lost their best friend? *More than a best friend, really,* he thought. How could anyone put into words the feelings that had swarmed through him whilst watching the video? And he was just an outsider looking in. He certainly couldn't, and it would be an insult to both Sarah and Gulliver to try. And so, he said nothing.

As if on cue, he heard Sarah's stomach rumble, breaking the spell that seemed to have been cast between them.

She smiled ruefully at him. "Time for my breakfast now! Goodbye Captain."

And without a backward glance, she slid off her chair and gracefully skipped down the stairs to the officer's mess, leaving Henry alone with his thoughts.

Sarah

Two days later, Sarah woke with a feeling of calm within her, for the first time in as long as she could remember. She had a sense that her constantly anxiety-ridden self was offering a cease fire, and allowing her to finally feel at peace. It was an unusual feeling, and she lay in bed mulling over the new sensation of waking without fear, and without the overwhelming shroud of heartache and grief.

It had been just over a month since she held her beloved Gulliver in her arms and watched him slip away from her, the day that her life changed forever. It had also been just over a month since she had last seen her toxic husband, and with the knowledge that she was safe, that he couldn't possibly find her where she was, she was beginning to feel her protective instincts relax. And she thought, with a tentative smile breaking through, *it is not an unwelcome feeling!* The real Sarah that she had hidden for so long, the Sarah that actually had feelings and opinions, was very slowly starting to emerge again. She was beginning to remember who she was, and she knew that part of the reason was because she was currently living the most extraordinary adventure!

She had not shared anything about herself with anyone else for years. It had become habit to keep herself to herself, and aside from Kelly, who had merely stated what everyone else seemed to already know, the captain, Henry, was the first person she had spoken openly with in a very long time. She thought she would feel guilt for sharing or be struck down with indescribable grief when talking about Gulliver and Uncle James, but she hadn't felt like that at all. Henry's quiet presence next to her and his calm demeanour had encouraged her to share. And the more she talked, the more she felt like a weight was being lifted from her.

"Yes," she said out loud, "I actually found the whole process surprisingly therapeutic."

Pushing back the covers, and with a spring in her step, she quickly changed and headed down to the officers' mess for breakfast. She always liked to be on time for the cook. He was waiting for her, and she eagerly eyed up the toasted English muffins dripping in butter with perfectly poached eggs sitting on top.

"Perfect timing as always, Sarah," said the cook, placing her breakfast in front of her.

"I could never be late for your food!" she replied, her eyes shining back at him in thanks for another delicious meal.

Licking her lips, and feeling contentedly full, she called out her thanks to the cook who was singing away to himself in the gally, and made her way out on to the deck. It was time to feed the horses.

"Sarah, there you are," called out the captain, hastily making his way over to her. "Come with me," he gestured, as he hurried straight past her to the railings on the side of the ship and pointed out into the ocean. "Dolphins!"

And as she cast her eyes over the sparkling blue water an elegant dolphin broke through the surface, and exposing itself in all its glory, launched into the air in a spectacular jump. And then another, and another appeared.

"How beautiful," Sarah cried out, not taking her eyes off them. "I've never seen real life dolphins before!"

Watching the exuberant pod, living wild and free, with the warmth of the sun on her back, coupled with the icy droplets landing on her skin from the ocean spray, Sarah felt like she was in paradise. The family of dolphins leapt, jumped and effortlessly swam alongside the ship for a gratifying ten whole minutes. When her private dolphin display finally ended, she turned to Henry and found his eyes quietly resting on her.

"There's nothing quite like it, is there?" he stated. "Seeing them in their natural world. I must have seen them a hundred times, but the sight of them never fails to stop me running over to watch them like an excited young boy! I find them truly captivating."

"They are just breath-taking to watch," agreed Sarah heartily. "And they have given me a memory that I will treasure forever. Thank you."

Her open enthusiasm was rewarded with a beaming smile from Henry, and she acknowledged, for the first time, how clear and bright his blue eyes were, how thick his neatly cropped dark hair was, and how toned the muscles of his caramel tanned arms were. She felt herself involuntary blush at the sudden unprofessional thoughts flashing through her mind, and swiftly dropped his gaze for fear of him noticing.

Following her lead, Henry looked back out to the vast expanse of ocean surrounding them, before replying, "I'm so pleased." And then with a subtle softness lining his voice, he added, "I too, shall treasure this memory."

They stood, leaning against the railings of the ship, side by side in companionable silence. Sarah realised that aside from the horses, this was the first time she had felt completely relaxed in another person's company in a very long time. There was something about the captain, with his calm, confident demeanour, and his quiet, unobtrusive ways that had somehow penetrated through her self-protective defensiveness. She noticed how they were not touching, but they were so very close. She could smell the subtle scent of his musky aftershave; she could feel the hairs on her arms prickling and a tingle under her skin at being in such close proximity to him.

"I really must go and feed the horses now," she blurted. "Thank you for the dolphin show." And with a brief smile she strode over to the entrance of the horses' hold, and without looking back at him, she slipped inside to her safe space. Her comfort zone with the horses. A place where she could settle her mind and attempt to process the overwhelming emotions that had overflowed inside her, seemingly completely out of the blue.

Sarah put herself straight to work. Her morning routine allowed her to empty her mind and focus only on tending to the horses. After feeding, mucking out and laying down fresh straw beds for the horses, scrubbing all the feed and water buckets and tidying the makeshift feed store, two hours had passed, and Sarah finally felt ready to begin the process of facing up to her newly blossoming feelings. Armed with her grooming box she slipped into Demeter and Persephone's stall. Sandwiched between the two mares, under the relaxing, rhythmical brush strokes, she let her mind wander.

She closed her eyes, inhaled the sweet smell of the horses, and felt gratitude wash over her for the place she was in in, right here, right now. How lucky she felt to be living such an extraordinary adventure. "Me!" she whispered into Demeter's ear. "Little old me working with horses on board a real-life cargo ship, in the middle of the ocean! Sometimes it all just feels like a dream," she admitted to the horse. "A wonderful, wonderful dream." Her heart then began to ache with the pain of losing Gulliver, and she knew that no dream could cause such sorrow, no amount of imagination could cause her such surmountable grief. "And that is why I know it's really happening. That I'm really here."

It dawned on her that in a few days' time they would arrive in South Africa. She would have to say goodbye to the beautiful mares she now called her friends. "Another loss," she said in a thick voice, burying her face in Demeter's mane. She would have to say goodbye to Henry, and she would have to face the chaos she had left behind. Heavy sobs began to pour out of her, and wrapping her arms tightly around the gentle mare, she allowed them to freely flow.

After a few moments, she felt Persephone nudging her. It was her turn to be groomed. She relaxed her arms from Demeter and dried her eyes inelegantly on the back of her hand. Turning to Persephone, she smiled at the mare. "You're absolutely right. It's time to focus. Crying isn't going to fix my life for me. It's time to make a plan."

Rhythmically brushing Persephone, with a newfound determination sweeping through her, she faced her feelings about Henry. She liked him. She instantly felt better for acknowledging the truth. He had been kind to her, welcomed her on board his ship and he had looked after her for the duration of their journey.

It was understandable that she would feel something towards him after so many years of being physically and emotionally abused by Julian. *He's also very handsome!* she allowed herself to admit. But she would be leaving him in a few days. She would be flying home to England, and he would continue his globe-trotting life at sea, and that was all there was to it. She knew she would never see him again. How could they possibly ever bump into each other again when she had absolutely no idea where she was going to end up in England and he was off travelling the world? There was also the small matter that she was still actually married. *Hopefully not for long,* she thought, desperately wanting to end all contact with Julian as soon as possible. But technically she was still a married woman. And then it dawned on her that she had no idea if Henry was married, or if he had a significant other. He had not divulged such information and she had not thought to ask. But knowing that she would never be seeing him again, she mused, *it doesn't really matter anyway.* Henry, just being Henry, had allowed her to feel again. Allowed her to think that another relationship might actually be possible. That she could feel fluttering of attraction again. She could be open to the possibility of letting someone into her life again, and for that, she would always be grateful to him. And she acknowledged that Henry had done a lot more for her than just being a kind boss. Her little budding crush for him would stay just that. A private surge of emotions that she could look back on, in many months to come, and remember the enchanting captain and his horses.

Her new positive take on life was buzzing through her veins, and she was resolved. She had been numb for so many years. By protecting herself, she had closed off her emotions, and she was beginning to realise that by doing so, not only had she blocked out her feelings of hurt and pain, but also feelings of joy, excitement, and love. She would now welcome such feelings, and she would embrace them. She would not be going back to her old life. Her new life was just starting. And as daunting as it was, she knew that there was a life out there waiting for her, she just needed the gumption to go out and get it.

"This is just the beginning," she said out loud to the horses. And seemingly out of nowhere a memory flashed before her eyes. She and Uncle James were sitting in the sunshine, eating ice-creams and watching the crashing waves roll over the golden sand of their favourite beach. She could see the familiar twinkle in his eyes as they laughed together. *Cornwall...* And then, to her surprise, "I'm moving to Cornwall," popped right out of her mouth.

Henry

Henry was tucking into a large plateful of beef wellington, roast potatoes and green beans with his fellow officers and Sarah. They were anchored up just outside the South African port of Cape Town and it was their last evening meal together before the space for his ship would be available and he could move her alongside the following morning. His crew were in great spirits that they had successfully survived the journey carrying such precious cargo, and they all agreed that it was down to Sarah and her excellent horsemanship skills. Sarah was wearing a bashful smile after receiving such high praise, something he thought she was not used to. Henry noted the flush of colour in her cheeks, giving her a warm glow, and he thought how pretty she looked in her simple white cotton shirt and denim shorts with her thick honey-coloured hair hanging loosely around her shoulders.

"You have outdone yourself, Cook," exclaimed Henry, licking his lips after the delicious feast.

"Thank you, Captain. And for pudding, Sarah's favourite!"

The crew erupted into affectionate cheering, knowing full well what was now to follow their beef wellington.

"I think I have perfected it now, Sarah!" said the cook, as he doled out generous helpings of treacle sponge pudding with custard. He handed the first bowl to Sarah and looked expectantly at her. Henry watched her take the first bite, the cook not taking his eyes off her.

"Cook!" she exclaimed. "It's better than mine! It's delicious, thank you so much."

More cheering commenced and Henry enjoyed watching the cook receive his much-deserved praise for the great effort he had put into their celebratory meal.

The merriment continued and light-hearted conversation flowed effortlessly around the table. Henry relaxed into the easy-going atmosphere, and like many times before, felt gratitude for his job, his crew, and his ship. And Sarah.

And Sarah. Watching her chatting away to the second mate, her eyes dancing and her hands gesticulating wildly, it was evident that she was narrating something of great amusement, because in that very moment, the second mate burst out laughing. The evening naturally dwindled to an end when the chief mate announced that he must take his leave and head up to the bridge. Thanks were offered to the cook as everyone got up to get back to work. Henry followed Sarah up the steps until they reached their cabin deck, and after swiftly admitting to himself that he did not yet want to leave her company, he asked, "Would you like to join me in my cabin for a drink before we turn in for the evening?"

"Yes, thank you," she replied.

She followed him inside his cabin, and he gestured for her to take a seat whilst he busied himself with getting her a drink.

"Ginger beer or lemonade?" he asked.

"Lemonade, please."

Handing her over the drink, he chose a ginger beer for himself and then settled himself in the chair opposite her. He was quite unsure where to start, a most unusual feeling for him, but he had noticed that as time had gone on, he was finding himself somewhat flustered in Sarah's company.

"I've had the most wonderful adventure," offered Sarah, breaking the silence.

"I must admit, I had my doubts about carrying horses across the Atlantic Ocean! But thanks to you," he said, smiling at her, "it has all gone smoothly. Thank you, Sarah, I really appreciate how you have looked after the horses so well in such, well, in such unusual conditions!"

"I also had my doubts," she admitted, "but Kelly, Martin's sister-in-law, assured me that I could do it." She smiled bashfully at him, then continued. "I'm so pleased she persuaded me to take the job."

With the ice now broken between them, their conversation flowed easily, and he listened quietly as Sarah talked about the horses. *She's so passionate about them*, he thought, as she delved into their individual personalities, and how much she was going to miss them.

"Sorry!" she exclaimed. "Once I get started on horses I can babble on for ages!"

Henry didn't mind in the least; he was quite content listening to her soft voice in the stillness of his quiet cabin.

"And what about you? What made you decide that you wanted to spend your life at sea?" she asked him with querying eyes, showing him that she was genuinely keen to learn why someone might choose to lead such a unique lifestyle.

He started from the beginning, and once he began to tell his tale he found her restful presence, her eagerly listening ear, an invitation to express the real him. He shared things that he had never shared with anyone before. He explained about the unexplainable pull that lured him to the sea. He told her about the burning desire within him that gave him the drive within him to succeed. The inner need to keep climbing the ladder until he had finally reached his goal of becoming a captain. And then, maybe because he was caught up in the moment, maybe because it was time, maybe because this alluring woman before him allowed him to be himself, then he told her the final moments he'd spent with his mother. And not just of his achievement, but also the feelings he'd experienced when climbing aboard his first ship as the captain with his mother on his arm, and the private elation they had both felt, and expressed once they had closed his cabin door and enjoyed the moment together. He divulged the utter devastation he had suffered at losing his mother. The all-consuming sorrow that had engulfed him. His moment of glory so short-lived because he could no longer share it with her.

He felt Sarah's hand lightly rest on his own in a momentary gesture of comfort. She removed her hand as quickly as she had placed it on his. She said nothing, but he knew that sometimes words were not needed. Sarah, of all people, understood the colossal depths one could delve into when swimming against the tide of grief. Although he felt a brief flush of embarrassment for openly sharing so much with her, it was short lived. Of all the people he could have chosen to open up to, he knew, in that very moment, that he would only have wanted it to be Sarah. The mysterious woman sitting across from him. She had confided in him about the loss of her uncle, and of her beloved horse, but there was something else. He couldn't begin to fathom what it might be, but there was a hauntingly sad look about her at times. He noticed when she thought no one was looking, that a heaviness would engulf her that she seemed to struggle to shake off. Over the past month she had blossomed, but there was still something. Something that made him know she was safe to share his thoughts with and that she would never judge or ridicule him.

It was getting late, and as much as he didn't want her to leave, they both had a busy day ahead of them tomorrow and it wasn't fair of him to keep her any longer. He stood up, and walked over to his desk, and after rummaging inside his top draw, he produced his last bag of wine gums. He did not want their parting to be without a kind gesture, and if anyone were to appreciate his treasured sweets, it would be Sarah.

"Try these," he offered, giving her the bag. "Moroccan sweets. I think you will find they are nothing like anything you have ever tasted."

Accepting the sweets, she replied, "Thank you. And thank you for a lovely evening. Goodnight, Captain."

He watched her walk away from him, but this time, she stopped, turned, and offered him a warm smile before leaving him alone in his cabin.

Henry settled himself back in his chair with another ginger beer, and this time he'd added a generous glug of whiskey. *Is it because I know I will never see her again?* he asked himself as he struggled to understand how he had just managed to confide such deeply hidden emotions to someone. *Is it because she too has suffered such loss? Or is it because I have never met anyone quite like her? And that she is stirring up emotions inside me that no woman ever has before?*

He briefly wished that Martin was with him so he could ask his opinion on this somewhat surreal situation. Martin was surprisingly astute when it came to reading other people and understanding body language, and Henry had benefitted from his wisdom with regards to previous crew members before. But the idea of discussing Sarah was swiftly dashed, for he knew that he would never ask Martin such a thing.

He looked over to the empty chair where she had been sitting just ten minutes ago, and he wondered what it might be like for her to rest her head against his shoulder. What it would be like to run his hands through her golden mane of hair and hold her in his arms.

He closed his eyes and thought of Louisa. Dear sweet-hearted Louisa. A surge of guilt swept over him as he did so. He had not thought of her since he climbed aboard his ship in Tenerife and set sail for Morocco. The indescribable feelings he held for Sarah, a woman he barely knew, he admitted he had not felt for her. He had settled for her kindness and generous support during his grief at losing his mother, and he had allowed her to believe that his feelings for her were honest, and that the future was available for them to share. But he realised now that he had not been truthful to her, or himself. He had never felt the deep yearning that he now felt for Sarah. A desire that he could not describe, but it was there. Just like his indescribable pull to be at sea.

The irony was that Louisa had been there for him, for years, waiting for him. Wanting him. Willing him to want her back, something he regretfully couldn't do. And now the likelihood of him ever seeing Sarah again was slim to zero when she stepped off his ship tomorrow morning. Acknowledging this, he felt awash with sadness. And he had to admit that in all honesty, he didn't have a clue as to any feelings Sarah held towards him. There had been a moment, he thought, when they were watching the dolphins. He couldn't put his finger on it, but he had sensed something between them when a wistful look had crossed over Sarah's face just for a second. And of course, they had both shared their stories of loss. But Henry could not be sure that Sarah had chosen him specifically, or if she was the sort of woman who shared openly in general. He desperately hoped it was the former, because for him, sharing with her had most definitely been a private, almost intimate affair, meant just for her. He held onto his inner voice, a voice that he trusted and usually held him in good stead, a voice that told him that she was like him. Careful with her feelings and even more careful with whom she chose to share them with.

He topped up his ginger beer and whiskey, slipped his shoes off and rested his feet on the empty chair, when a thought suddenly occurred to him. *I won't ever see her again after she steps off my ship tomorrow...* He stalled, not daring to voice his idea even to himself. He took a large sip of his whiskey. *Maybe if I could come up with a way of keeping her in my life, at least just for a little while longer, it might give me time to work out if this is just some kind of infatuation., After all, the past month has been most unusual, even for me! Or if it is something more? And if Sarah shows no indication of wanting a continuation of our friendship than I'll know for sure. And I definitely won't ever have to see her again if she declines!*

Feeling slightly buoyed with his new plan, Henry glanced at his clock. He was to meet Bartholomew Cooper, the shipping company's owner, in just four hours. It was definitely time for him to turn in for the night.

Sarah

Through bleary eyes Sarah swung her arm out from under her warm duvet and fumbled until she managed to find her phone so she could switch the bleeping alarm off. As soon as she flicked it off, it started again.

"Arghhhh, ok, ok, I'm getting up," she said out loud.

Focusing on her phone, she peered at the screen to make sure she clicked the alarm off properly, and then she saw it.

Be Strong.

Be positive.

Your life is just beginning.

Cornwall will be your new home.

She re-read her own words again within the message she had attached to her alarm last night. The memory of being cocooned in Henry's cabin last night came flooding back. The two of them had talked into the twilight hours and his words, so eloquently spoken and showing his vulnerability, had stirred something within her. Listening to his story unfold and learning of his own heartache, coupled with the tenderness he had shown her down in the horses' hold when she was seasick, she knew that her once simmering little crush was now bubbling fiercely inside her. She remembered placing her hand on his during a moment of her own weakness. She had desperately wanted to place her arm around his shoulders and comfort him, but she knew that would have been inappropriate and would cross the invisible boundary between them. Today she would be flying back to England, and she would have to say goodbye to her captain. She read her message again, pleased that she'd had the foresight to remind herself that although her adventure was now coming to an end, she had much to look forward to. With gritty determination, she hauled herself out of bed and into the bathroom. Looking into the mirror, directly into her own eyes, she spoke out loud. "You will be brave, and you will get through this. Cornwall is waiting for you."

She skipped down to the officer's mess, and as usual, the cook was waiting for her.

"Good morning, Sarah."

"Good morning, Cook," she replied, eyeing up the bacon sandwich he was holding in front of her. "For me?"

"Of course, Sarah." She watched the cook place down her breakfast before turning to her, his eyes full of emotion, and he enveloped her in a ginormous hug. "I shall miss you Sarah," he gushed.

Returning his embrace, she replied, "I'll miss you too, Cook. You have been a real friend to me over the past month. Thank you for looking after me."

Releasing her from his arms, he returned to his usual bubbly self. "And every time I make treacle sponge pudding, I shall think of you! I must get back to my kitchen. Goodbye, Sarah." And he was gone.

Sarah smiled to herself as she tucked into her delicious breakfast. The cook really had been her friend. He had looked out for her and always made sure she had plenty to eat. She was going to miss his kindness and upbeat, happy-go-lucky personality. She knew she would always look back on him fondly.

Sarah spent the next hour preparing the horses for the final leg of their journey. They were to be loaded into a crate, lifted out of the hold, and finally back on to dry land, then moved onto a horse lorry for the one-hour journey to their new home.

In what seemed like no time at all, Sarah was closing the latch on the crate and giving the signal to the chief mate that the horses were safely loaded. She hurried up on deck and watched the huge crane haul the horses onto the quay. They were now on South African land.

Although she had promised herself that she would shed no tears for leaving Henry, she made no such promise about being parted from the horses. She knew they were not hers. Right from the start, they were just her charges for the month, but that didn't mean she wasn't sad to let them go. They had become her friends and confidantes and saying goodbye to any friend was always a hardship. She felt her tears trickling down her cheeks and reminded herself that the four mares were about to begin their own new adventure, just like she was.

She made her way back up to her cabin to finish packing her things. A car would be collecting her soon to take her to the airport. Henry's cabin door was slightly ajar. She could hear two men deep in conversation. She recognised Henry's voice straight away, but the other she was not familiar with. And then she heard Henry say, "I can't make that decision Sir, I'm afraid you will have to ask her yourself."

"But my wife said she needs her," replied the mysterious voice. "And you just said yourself how fantastic she is."

Sarah was hovering outside her own door. She couldn't help but hear them, but she knew that no good ever came from eavesdropping, so she was doing her best to block out what she presumed was a private conversation. She noisily opened her door to alert them that they were no longer alone.

"Ah, here she is now," she heard Henry announce. "You can ask her."

"Sarah, would you mind stepping in my cabin for a moment please?"

Intrigued to find out it was her that they were discussing, Sarah tentatively peeked around Henry's door. "Hello," she said to the two men looking back at her.

"Come in, come in," said Henry. "This is Mr Cooper, the shipping company's owner. He'd like to speak with you."

The mystery man came straight over to her, grasped her hand in his and shook it warmly in greeting. "So good to finally meet you, Sarah. I'm Barty. My captain has been keeping me updated on the horses' well-being and I have heard nothing but high praise for your fine horsemanship skills and capabilities."

Slightly taken aback with being greeted by Henry's boss with such enthusiasm, Sarah tried to compose herself, before replying, "Thank you. Your horses have been a pleasure to care for."

"I'll get straight to the point," said Barty. "My wife, Caroline, would very much like for you to accompany the horses to our home, and stay with us to help them settle in. You have spent a month in very close quarters with the horses and Caroline thinks that your presence will be most valuable for the horses' wellbeing whilst they get used to their new home, and Caroline as their new owner. You will of course be paid for the extra time spent in South Africa."

"How long for?" stammered Sarah, trying to take in this new turn of events.

"Caroline suggested a week. So, you'll do it?" replied Barty eagerly.

Seeing as she didn't actually have anywhere to go when she set foot back in England, Sarah thought an extra week in South Africa might give her a chance to come up with some sort of plan. Plus she would get to meet Caroline, the horses' new owner, and see their new home.

"Ok," she said simply.

"Wonderful!" exclaimed Barty. "And Henry, you are to set sail for Thailand in five days. My wife absolutely insists you come for dinner the night before! She would like to thank you personally for bringing her horses safely home. Now why don't you take Sarah to the horse lorry. I'll meet you at my cars afterwards." And smiling brightly at them both, he hurried out of Henry's cabin to go and see his new boy's toys.

"He's a bit of a whirlwind, isn't he?" giggled Sarah nervously.

"Indeed, he is! Are you sure you're ok with this?" Henry asked her gently. "He really put you on the spot. You don't have to go if you don't want to. I'll speak to him if you would like me to?"

"Thank you, I really appreciate the offer, but it's fine. I'd like to meet Caroline, and this will give me a chance to settle the horses into their new home."

"It's agreed then," replied Henry. "We'd better go. Mr Cooper doesn't like to be kept waiting!"

Sarah rushed into her cabin and hurriedly stuffed the last of her bits and pieces into her small case, all the while her heart beating ten to the dozen about the new change of plans, and also the realisation that she would be seeing Henry again in a few days' time when he came for dinner. Today would not be their final goodbye after all.

Henry took her case, and she followed him, for the last time, down the four flights of stairs and out on to the deck. She turned around in a full circle to get one last look at the ship that had been her home for the past month. "Goodbye," she whispered. With Henry still leading the way, she followed him down the gangplank and onto the busy dock yard. Machinery and men were hard at work and as Sarah now realised, the business of shipping was permanently on the go.

The horses had already been loaded onto the horse lorry by the time they arrived. Sarah looked up at the huge, gleaming white, and hugely expensive horse lorry. She had never seen anything like it. Barty and his wife really did make sure no expense was spared for these horses. She was pleased the mares would be travelling in such a safe vehicle and would be kept as comfortable as possible with the padded stalls and hi-tech air-conditioning unit.

She watched Henry open the passenger side door, climb in, place her case inside, then speak to the driver.

"He's ready to go," announced Henry, climbing back down so he was now facing her. "Thank you for everything, Sarah. We couldn't have done this without you."

"And thank you, Captain, for the trip of a lifetime!"

Sarah felt an awkwardness descend upon them both, neither of them seemingly knowing how to say goodbye. Sarah would have welcomed it if Henry were to behave like the cook, to envelop her in his arms, squeeze her tight and tell her he would miss her. But she knew that was not his way. What had felt so natural with the cook, would not now, in this very moment, feel natural with the captain. Sarah held out her hand, and in a split second she felt Henry clasp hers in both of his own. She smiled up at him, relieved that she had made the correct gesture, and said, "I'll see you in a few days, Captain."

"I look forward to it," replied Henry, releasing her hand, and standing back for her to climb into the huge lorry. "Goodbye, Sarah."

Sarah was lost in her own world during the journey from the dockyard all the way to Barty's house. As the huge lorry weaved its way down Barty's spectacular driveway, she realised that 'home' for Barty and Caroline could actually be described as a millionaire's holiday mansion for the rest of the world's population. They had left the dusty African road behind them. His perfectly tarmacked two-mile-long drive was lined with palm trees and exotic flowers. Green grass paddocks divided with immaculate post and rail fences lined one side of the driveway, and on the other side, was a vast expanse of what looked like their own private beach. Miles of golden sand stretched out before her, and the South African waves were gently crashing on the shoreline. And the stables, she had never in her life seen a yard like it. From high up in the cab of the lorry, she could see eight large and airy stables, a huge tack room and feed room, an open barn filled to the brim with hay and straw, and the icing on the cake, a full-sized schooling area. Sarah felt like she had just stepped into horse heaven.

As the driver brought the lorry to a halt on the yard, a pretty middle-aged lady came skipping out of the tack room. Waving enthusiastically, she called out, "Welcome, welcome. I can't believe you're finally here!"

Before Sarah's feet had even touched the ground, she had been pulled into a welcoming embrace by the friendly lady.

"You must be Sarah. I'm Caroline. It is so good to finally meet you. I'm so pleased you agreed to come to our home. Thank you."

"It's lovely to meet you, Caroline," said Sarah whilst she extracted herself from her arms. "Should I unload the horses now?"

"Absolutely not!" said Caroline. "You must be exhausted. You must rest." She pulled Sarah over to the wooden bench outside the tack room. "Forgive me for being a bad host but I must stay whilst the grooms unload and settle the horses. Once I know my girls are safe and sound, I'll take you to the house where you can freshen up," she said, beaming down at her.

Sarah watched as three grooms appeared and set to work with the horses. Sarah had not known what to expect. Deep down she had wondered if the super-duper rich Caroline would be a little bit snobby, but now having met her, she felt guilty of such a thought. Caroline was like a warm, welcoming puppy dog. And her eagerness to make sure her horses were looked after correctly told Sarah all she needed to know. The mares she had come to love over the past month would want for nothing, and they would be utterly adored by their new devoted owner.

After two days of relaxing and being treated like a queen by Caroline, who was almost generous to a fault, Sarah continued to be awed by Barty and Caroline's exquisite mansion home, which also included a private swimming pool with a beautiful fountain in the middle and Caribbean-style outdoor bar. And the views! Sarah felt like she could just lose herself in the gorgeous stretch of empty golden sands and clear blue ocean. She had been right - the beach lining the property belonged to the Coopers. And the moment she had been waiting for arrived when Caroline tentatively asked her if she thought Diana might be ready to be ridden in the sand school. Keen to finally be allowed to do what she was being paid for, Sarah had immediately said yes.

Caroline told her that Diana felt like the horse she had bonded with the most, and she would be the one she would like to ride first. Sarah prepared Diana and led her into the school for her new owner's first ride. The patient mare waited quietly whilst Caroline mounted and got herself ready, and a groom must have turned on the music system when an upbeat radio song rang out into the quiet air. The highly trained horse followed Caroline's gentle cues to the letter. Walk to trot transitions, trot to canter transitions, twenty-meter circles and she even executed a lovely half pass from Caroline's somewhat muddled request. Caroline trotted Diana over to Sarah and grinned down like a Cheshire cat. "Isn't she just the most wonderful horse!"

Returning her smile, Sarah agreed that she was indeed the most perfect horse.

"Would you like to ride her?" offered Caroline.

"Yes please! I'd never turn down a ride on one of your mares!"

In no time at all, Sarah was sitting comfortably in Diana's beautiful handmade leather saddle. Sarah set off for a gentle trot around the school to get a feel for Diana. As she expertly followed her cues, just like she had done for Caroline, Sarah heard 'Don't Stop Believin'' by The Journey pour out of the speakers.

"One of my favourites!" she told the horse. "Come on Diana, let's see what you've got." And with the familiar musical notes in her ear, Sarah and Diana danced. To the beat of the music, Diana performed perfect transitions between collected trot and extended trot. She excelled in her canter and flying changes and Sarah knew that just like it had been with Persephone, she could ask for more. She steadied the mare and asked for a piaffe. She and Diana focused on the intricate steps, building with the crescendo of the music, and then in one fluid movement Diana executed the perfect levade. When all four hooves were back on the ground, Sarah heard clapping and cheering from the edge of the ring. She had not realised at first, but it was no longer just Caroline spectating. She had been joined by the three grooms, two gardeners and Barty.

"Sarah, wow, that was fantastic!" Caroline cried out.

"Henry was certainly right about you!" called out Barty. "He told us you were amazing, didn't he Caroline," he said, turning to his wife who was still beaming up at Sarah.

"Let's sit on the terrace and have a celebratory drink!" announced Barty.

"Absolutely," agreed Carline, nodding enthusiastically at her husband's idea.

"I'll see you up there," replied Sarah. "I'll just put Diana away." She watched the staff return to their duties and Barty and Caroline, hand in hand, strolled off to their poolside terrace. Sarah was grateful for the peace and quiet. The mention of Henry suddenly brought her unruly emotions to the surface again and she needed a moment alone to regain control. In two days, she would be seeing him again. She had tried not to think about him. She had tried to push him far out of her thoughts, but it was futile knowing that she would be seeing him again very soon. And so she decided that she would allow herself to feel just a little bit excited about seeing him again. She would have the rest of her life to push him out of her thoughts. She might as well enjoy the butterflies fluttering around inside her until their final parting in forty-eight hours' time.

Henry

After spending three nights in a modest hotel room, Henry was thrilled to be climbing aboard his ship again. As he stepped onto the gang plank, he saw Martin hurrying along the deck to greet him.

"Welcome aboard, Captain!"

"Thank you, Chief," replied Henry, greeting Martin with a hearty handshake. The two men slapped each other affectionately on the back.

Henry and Martin chatted away as they made their way up the six flights of stairs to the captain's cabin. Henry retrieved two ice-cold beers out of his fridge, handed one to Martin and gestured for his friend to sit down.

"All well on the voyage down, Chief?" asked Henry.

"Smooth sailing all the way apart from a minor thirty-six hours of no sleep during a particularly brutal storm. But nothing to worry about, we've been in worse!"

"Yes, we caught the tail end of it, only a little bit bumpy for us but poor Sarah didn't fare quite so well. Sick as a dog she was!" replied Henry, picturing a green-looking Sarah lying in her makeshift cabin bed down with the horses.

"Oh no!" exclaimed Martin. "Is she ok now?"

"Absolutely. As soon as we left the storm she bounced right back."

"And how did she do?" asked Martin tentatively, fully aware that she came on his sister-in-law's recommendation.

Henry smiled broadly at him. "Martin, I can honestly tell you that she was fantastic. From the moment she arrived, those horses were in the most capable hands, and she was definitely the best woman for the job. I must thank you for your quick thinking and arranging her to be my horse trainer."

Henry saw Martin physically relax on hearing such praise for Sarah, for he knew that his opinion on Sarah would also be a reflection on his brother and sister-in-law regarding their choice of recommendation. He was deeply pleased that he could genuinely express to Martin his highest regard for Sarah.

"I'm looking forward to meeting her this evening," announced Martin.

"When will you be meeting her?" asked Henry, curious to know why and how such an arrangement had been made without his knowing.

"With you, at Barty's house, didn't he tell you? As soon as he found out it was me who organised Sarah to work for him, his wife insisted that I join you all."

"So, we will both get to see the lair of the playboy for ourselves!" jested Henry.

Chuckling along with Henry at their inside joke, the chief announced that he must get back to work. There was much to do before their night off. He added a passing comment as he stepped outside Henry's cabin. "Don't forget, Barty wants us dressed in our uniform to show us off to his wife!"

Henry's day passed quickly. As usual, before setting sail on a new voyage, he was swamped with paperwork. Forms and lists had to be checked and signed, confirming that all the cargo was present and correct and that the necessary supplies were fully stocked for his crew. Then he had to meet with his chief engineer to ensure that all was as it should be in his engine room. He felt the familiar buzz inside him that he would soon be travelling again to pastures new.

Henry had just slipped his arms into his handmade doeskin captain's jacket when he heard Martin calling him. "The car's here, Captain. Are you ready?"

"Yes, Chief, I'm on my way."

Looking at himself in the mirror, he gave himself a determined nod. He had vowed to himself that he would not part from Sarah without giving her some inclination of his feelings towards her. Preferably he would like to get her on her own and voice his thoughts directly, but if not, he would revert to plan B. He would pick his moment carefully and then.... "Well," he said out loud to himself, "I'll just have to wait and see what this evening brings." He patted his inside pocket gently to make sure it was definitely in there. It was.

Both Henry and Martin were equally impressed with the size, style and elegance of Barty and Caroline's home. The fact that they had more money than they knew what to do with was very apparent, but Henry had to admit it, they had class.

They were met by the family butler and escorted to the outdoor terrace where Barty, decked out in his black-tie evening suit, greeted them warmly.

"Captain, Chief, welcome. Take a seat and enjoy our spectacular view whilst I fix us some drinks. The ladies are running a little late I'm afraid. In fact, look," said Barty, pointing over to his beach. "There they are now."

Henry cast his eyes over to where Barty was pointing, and there, on the open stretch of private beach, were two horse riders. Caroline and Sarah were galloping across the sand with the majestic grey horses powering through the breaking waves. Henry was transfixed by Sarah. Watching her ride never failed to fascinate him. And seeing her ride with such abandon, such speed and grace, empowered him to fulfil his evening plan for the evening. He could not imagine never seeing this remarkable woman again.

"She is something special, is she not?" asked Barty, drawing Henry's attention away from Sarah and back into the present conversation with Barty and Martin.

"Your wife is a wonderful rider, Mr Cooper," Henry replied carefully.

"Barty, please, Henry. We are in my home! No need for such formalities here. And I did not mean my wife, I already know how wonderful she is."

Henry felt Barty's eyes on him, and for a split second he sensed that Barty could read his mind like an open book. And then the look was gone, and Barty reverted to his usual eccentric self. Henry could not deny Sarah's capabilities and simple replied with honesty, "Yes, Barty, Sarah is uniquely gifted with horses, I have never seen anyone connect with a horse like she does."

"Caroline and I had the privilege of watching her the other day. The way she made Diana dance, it was like she had cast a magical spell over her, I have never seen anything like it. Even at all the fancy horse shows my wife insists I attend with her!"

The three men chatted amicably amongst themselves whilst sipping Barty's elaborate cocktails, and both Henry and Martin agreed that Barty was quite the host. They wanted for nothing. His natural generosity tumbled out of him, and his quick wit and clever mind made him excellent company.

"Darling, so sorry we're late," called out Caroline, breaking up the men's chatter and drawing their attention to the top of the marble steps as the ladies emerged from the mansion.

All three men stood up and stared as the two elegant women glided down the steps towards them. Henry noted that Caroline looked beautiful in her gold, knee-length cocktail dress, her eyes only on her husband as she sauntered towards him. And he was surprised to see that she was not some besotted twenty-year-old. She was a mature, stylish woman, close in age to Barty himself. Henry began to realise that there was a lot more to Barty than he, and the many newspaper articles, let on. But Henry felt his pulse quicken when he saw Sarah. Her navy-blue, floor-length silk dress shimmered as she walked. The delicate straps and scooped neckline effortlessly showed off her feminine figure, and her honey-blonde hair framed her beautiful features. Henry had never seen anyone look so exquisitely charming.

"Ladies, you're here! Now the party can really get started," said Barty, embracing his wife and affectionately kissing her on her cheek. Then he made his way over to his private bar, before mixing and shaking up an alcohol and fruit punch. "My own concoction," he announced, eagerly placing the drinks before them. Each glass contained an assortment of fresh fruit and was topped off with a little umbrella.

Raising their glasses, they clinked them together, praising Barty for his efforts. The conversation flowed continuously throughout the evening, as did Barty's cocktails, along with a constant stream of delicious nibbles. Henry, relaxed in his chair and enjoying the friendly atmosphere, felt himself suddenly focus when Barty brought Sarah to the forefront of the conversation.

"We've asked her to stay," Henry heard Barty tell Martin. "Caroline would love to have some more private lessons with her, as would some of her friends. She is the best after all. But alas," Barty said dramatically, "she is still set to leave in three days."

"I'm so sorry, Barty," chipped in Sarah, "and, I'm sure I'll regret saying this when I'm surrounded by grey skies and misty drizzle! But Cornwall is calling for me, and I must answer my call!"

"I know, I know," agreed Barty. "We're just going to miss you, aren't we Caroline?"

Caroline nodded enthusiastically. "Maybe I should have written her a terrible reference then she wouldn't have been offered the job and we could keep her!"

Barty, Caroline and Sarah all promptly burst out laughing, and Henry, for the first time that evening, felt excluded from the group. He looked at Martin, who merely shrugged his shoulders, equally out of the picture as he was.

As if sensing his unease, Sarah offered, "I'm moving to Cornwall when I leave South Africa. A job became available sooner than expected and Caroline was kind enough to write me a reference as my current employer. She must have said something nice about me because they said I can start next week!" she finished excitedly.

"Congratulations," replied Henry, with as much enthusiasm as he could muster. It had suddenly dawned on him that he didn't know anything about her life outside of his ship, and South Africa. He had been so focused on work, and Sarah in the here and now, he had not thought about where she was going or what she would do once she arrived back in England. Or even if she had a significant other waiting for her.

His thoughts were interrupted when Barty's butler announced the arrival of the car that was to take them back to the ship. He felt his heart plummet that his evening was finishing with even more confusion regarding Sarah than when he first arrived.

"Oh, can you hold on a minute?" Sarah blurted out, then she jumped up and scurried off towards the house and out of sight.

Caroline made her way over to Henry and Martin, hugged them warmly and thanked them for their wonderful company. She told them that they must visit again as soon as their ship returned to South Africa. Both Henry and Martin expressed their gratitude for such a lovely evening, and promised that they would indeed return. And then all eyes turned to Sarah as she hurried back towards them, a small package in her hand.

Slightly breathless, she held out her hand to Martin. "It has been so great to finally meet you! I can't wait to tell Kelly," she said sincerely.

"Will you be seeing her soon?" replied Martin.

"In a few weeks. She's going to come to Cornwall for a mini break as soon as I'm settled."

And then she turned to Henry. "For you, Captain." She handed him the brown paper package. As she looked up, directly into his eyes, Henry knew that this was his moment. With all eyes now on him, he felt eternally grateful that he had his plan B. He slipped his hands into his pocket and pulled out an envelope.

"Thank you," he said, indicating to the package. "And this is for you." Holding her gaze, he smiled warmly at her. "Goodbye, Sarah."

"Goodbye, Captain."

The butler ushered them towards the driveway, and after opening the car door, Henry turned back and saw her. She lifted up her hand and waved. His heart felt heavy. The butler coughed, politely indicating that it was time to go. He nodded towards Sarah, climbed into the car, and felt his heart sink as he was taken away from her.

Sarah

It was the evening of Sarah's final day, and she and Caroline were enjoying their last ride together. They were chatting contentedly, and Sarah was soaking up every wonderful minute of it for her memory bank. She knew that she would never forget this stunning private beach in South Africa and her welcoming hosts. The burning sun was slowly setting, offering her the most magnificent of African sun sets. The warm breeze gently blew through her hair and as silence descended between them, all she could hear was the sound of gentle waves lapping around Demeter's hooves.

"Shall we have one last gallop?" asked Caroline.

Beaming back at her friend, Sarah pushed Demeter into a brisk trot before replying, "Race you!" And she was gone. She could hear Caroline laughing behind her, and the thunder of Persephone's hooves as Caroline pushed her to catch up. She gave Demeter a lose rein and she ran. Sarah felt her heart surge with freedom as Demeter's powerful legs covered the open space before her effortlessly. For Sarah, nothing in this world could compete with the intoxicating sensations she felt when galloping at full speed. As Demeter continued to run, Sarah focused on her movement, and the way her mane flowed in the breeze, and she inhaled her sweet horsey smell, because she knew, in months to come, that she wanted this memory to be vivid and clear, to stimulate all of her senses, so she could relive this moment over and over again in her dreams.

Sarah reluctantly slowed Demeter down. They were almost at the boundary of Caroline's property, and Demeter was beginning to tire. Caroline rode up beside her, grinning from ear to ear, and with emotion audible in her voice, she said, "I'm really going to miss you, Sarah."

"I'm going to miss you too, and your horses," replied Sarah, her own voice thick with emotion, as they both turned their horses around for the long plod home.

Sarah's car arrived bright and early for her transfer to the airport, and after much hugging and shedding of heartfelt tears, Sarah climbed into the car and waved goodbye to her new friends, Caroline and Barty. She rummaged around in her handbag, pulled out the white paper bag of sweets that Henry had given her and popped one in her mouth. Resting her head against the window, she idly stared out of the window as the unusual mixture of sugar and spices hit her tastebuds. *These really are the most unusual, most delicious sweets I've ever tasted!*

Sarah had only ever travelled as what one might call 'cattle class,' but today, courtesy of Barty, she would be flying first class all the way to England. There was no waiting in queues, no being shoved and pushed by gazillions of other passengers, just a smooth transition from the car, through security and then she was escorted straight on to the plane where she was given a private booth for the duration of the journey.

Sarah settled herself down in the generously sized comfy seat, gratefully received the glass of sparkling orange juice the friendly air stewardess offered her and then closed her eyes. *This is it. I'm finally going home.* Once the plane was high up in the sky, and all the passengers were allowed to take off their seat belts and relax, Sarah delved into her cabin bag and pulled out the envelope that Henry had given her. She had read his letter over and over again, but she couldn't help herself from wanting to devour his words one more time.

Dear Sarah

I have very much enjoyed your company whilst on board my ship for this past month. Your work with the horses has been exemplary, and I will admit that you have opened my eyes to how truly wonderful these animals are, and for that, I thank you.

I think that my ship will seem somewhat empty without your company, something that I have now become accustomed to as well.

I would very much like to remain in contact with you, and I have enclosed my address if you would like to write to me. I can assure you that wherever I am in the world, the company always makes sure we get our mail!

Good luck with your new job.

Your friend

Henry

Sarah felt herself glowing from the inside out knowing that Henry wanted to stay in contact with her. He wanted to be her friend. And maybe, in time, she hoped, possibly something more. She was so pleased with herself for following her gut instinct with the present she gave Henry. Once Caroline explained to her that Barty's mini dinner party was to be a formal affair - any excuse for that man to dress up, Caroline had exclaimed, giggling about her husband's flamboyant ways - Sarah had expressed despair at her complete lack of anything remotely suitable to wear. Caroline had insisted on taking her to the local town for a shopping spree. It was whilst she was there that she noticed a little second-hand bookshop, and displayed in the window, right in front of her, was a first edition copy of Harper Lee's *To Kill A Mockingbird*. It was one of her favourites, and knowing what an avid reader Henry was, she had made an impulsive decision to buy him the book. As a thank you, she had justified to herself at the time, for all his kindness.

And after reading his words, she knew she had done the right thing. Henry would know that his letter of friendship was welcomed as soon as he saw the book; he would not have an agonising wait to receive her first letter to find her answer.

Sarah carefully folded her precious letter and placed it back in its envelope. After her early start, she could feel her eyelids growing heavy. She closed her eyes and as she slowly drifted off to sleep, she pictured Henry, so handsome and dashing in his smart captain's uniform.

On landing in England, Sarah and her fellow first-class passengers were efficiently and swiftly moved through security and passport control, probably before the rest of the regular passengers had even left the plane! *I could get used to this first class malarky*, she thought with a smile. Just as she was pondering on where she might find the coach station, she saw a smartly dressed man right outside the arrivals gate with her name printed on a large board. Intrigued, she ambled over to him and introduced herself. It transpired that Caroline had organised for a private driver to take her right to her new front door. Sarah felt a wave of gratitude, yet again, for the kindness that Barty and Caroline had bestowed on her.

In typical British style, as soon as she set foot outside of the airport, she was met with grey, misty drizzle. She laughed quietly to herself after the idle comment she had made to everyone at the dinner party. But rather than it dampening her spirits, she welcomed it. She was home.

It was dusk when the driver finally pulled up outside the little cottage that she would now be calling home. It was owned by the riding school she would be working for; the cottage was designated for the head rider and trainer. She had not been able to believe her luck when she found the advert five days ago. The stables were in desperate need for a new head rider due to their current one up and leaving them in the lurch, giving them no notice, just as the holiday season was about to begin. She had tentatively enquired and after both Caroline and Kelly emailed Tia, the yard owner, with glowing references for her, Tia had jumped at the chance to hire her. And the fact that the job came with accommodation within a one mile walk of the yard was the cherry on top.

Sarah stepped out of the car and inhaled the fresh countryside air. It even smelled like home! It was such a contrast from the South African air, so heavy with heat, dust and spices. The air of her homeland was rich and fresh with a delicate floral scent from the wild hedgerow flowers. She thanked her driver and waved goodbye to him, then picked up her case, opened the little wooden gate and stepped inside. A little crazy paved path led the way to her duck egg blue front door, and just as Tia had described, there was a broken terracotta plant pot next to the door. Lifting it up, she found the door key, and finally, she let herself into her home.

It was a typical Cornish country cottage both on the outside and inside. A comfy-looking squishy, threadbare sofa took centre stage of the little sitting room, positioned right in front of the stone-built fireplace. The teeny tiny kitchen was stocked with all the white goods she would need. She crept up the wooden staircase and found a generous-sized bedroom and a small, yet perfectly functional bathroom. That was it. *Tiny but perfect!*

Heading back downstairs, she noticed a gift basket left on the kitchen counter. It was filled with a loaf of bread, milk, butter, tea bags, a selection of cakes, and a little handwritten note.

Welcome to Elderberry Cottage.

Thought you might need a few bits to keep you going.

The local shop is in the village two miles away, I'll take you there tomorrow.

Looking forward to meeting you.

Tia.

Sarah smiled at the thoughtful gesture from Tia. She had a good feeling about her, and she was very much looking forward to meeting her and seeing her new workplace. Elderberry Riding School and training centre was a bustling equestrian hub. It was situated right next to the coastline. Nestled between the sand dunes, three miles away from the closest village, it was picture perfect Cornwall. They offered training in both jumping and dressage, as well as exhilarating gallops across the sand dunes and beach, and idle plods around the country lanes. There was something for everyone, be it local or holiday maker, beginner or advanced. And their horses were kept in tip top condition for whatever job they were required to do. Tia had informed her that the stables owned twenty-four horses in full work, plus the four private horses that belonged to Tia and the three girls who worked for her, and Gwendoline, a miniature Shetland pony who was the resident yard mischief maker! Sarah was certainly looking forward to meeting her!

She was exhausted from her long day, which she reminded herself had started in Africa! She took a chocolate brownie upstairs with her, climbed into her pyjamas and flopped into bed. She spent a few minutes pinging off emails to Kelly and Caroline to let them know that she had arrived safely, and before she had even managed to finish her brownie, she fell into a deep, restful sleep. Tomorrow was the start of her new life.

Henry

Henry was on the night shift. He was comfortably sitting in his control chair on the bridge looking out on a calm sea spread out beneath a clear twinkling night sky. It had been two weeks since he had set sail from Africa, and tomorrow, he would be docking his ship in Thailand. It had also been two weeks since he had given Sarah his letter. He had thought about her every single day he had been at sea. Every time he walked past the owner's cabin, on the way to his own, he felt a wave of disappointment that she was not there. Sometimes he pretended that she was behind the door, tucked up on the comfy chair, reading one of her beloved books. He picked up the copy of *To Kill A Mockingbird* and idly thumbed the pages, then he flicked through to the opening page and read Sarah's inscription for the hundredth time.

Dear Henry,

I saw this and thought of you.

It's one of my favourites.

I hope you enjoy it as much as I do.

Sarah

She had seen it and thought of him. Knowing that she had thought of him filled him with a warmth that flowed through his veins. It gave him confidence that he had done the right thing suggesting that they stayed in touch. And he desperately hoped that when he arrived in Thailand, and the crew's post was delivered to them, there would be a letter for him from Sarah. Taking his mind off the much-anticipated letter, Henry delved back into the world of 1930s Alabama, and Scout. He had enjoyed the book as a boy, but now knowing it was one of Sarah's favourites, he had a newfound enthusiasm for it and was keen to devour it from cover to cover.

At six o'clock in the morning, Henry and his chief guided his ship into the southern Thai harbour. The sun was shining, the ocean calm and his arrival into the port was smooth sailing. Henry had forty-eight hours for his ship to be unloaded, reloaded with cargo, then he would be off to Sydney, Australia. And he had an idea.

"Martin, any plans for the day?" enquired Henry.

"Not really," replied Martin, shrugging his shoulders. "I thought I'd pop into the local town for breakfast and write a post card to Kyle and Kelly. You?"

"I've had an idea!" announced Henry. "Let's do something a bit different. I've got to make a quick call, meet me on deck in half an hour!" And with a glint of mischief in his eyes, he hurried off to his cabin.

Henry accompanied Martin for breakfast, and chose a picturesque postcard for Sarah, crossing his fingers in the hope that he would receive a letter from her, and that it would include her new address. He had still not shared his idea with Martin for fear of him refusing to join him. After they had finished their breakfast at a little Thai café, Henry announced that they were to take a taxi to get to their destination.

"You have got to be kidding me!" blustered Martin when they pulled up outside a tourist riding stables. "Please tell me we are not doing what I think we are doing?"

Henry looked over at his friend's stricken face and grinned. "Yep, we're going riding."

They were greeted by a friendly English woman, who introduced herself as Ginny, the owner of the riding stables.

"Hello, I'm Henry, I spoke to you on the phone this morning. Thank you so much for fitting us in at such short notice, we only have a few hours of free time!"

"Absolutely no problem at all," replied Ginny. Then she turned to Martin who was looking a particularly iffy shade of green. "Your first ride?" she asked him.

Martin was still in too much shock to speak, so Henry intervened. "Yes, it's the first time for both of us."

"Don't worry," she said, smiling at Martin. "We often have people who have never ridden before, our horses are perfectly safe and very well trained. Now then," she said, eyeing them up. "Henry, you will ride Missy, and Martin, you will ride Bessie." A local Thai boy suddenly materialised leading two tacked up horses towards them.

Ginny explained to them the correct way to mount their steeds, and once safely on board, she elegantly mounted her own horse.

"I'm going to take you for a gentle walk along the beach. That's it. There will be no galloping!" she said with a chuckle. "I promise you; Missy and Bessie will plod along quietly behind my horse. That is their job, and they know it very well."

Henry hated to admit it, but both he and Martin were about as ungainly as a person could be for the first ten minutes of the ride. It was such an unusual feeling to be transported along by a living, breathing animal and it took them a while to settle into the beat of the horses' walk. But Ginny had been right. Missy and Bessie plodded along, thankfully without any direction given from the hapless novices. The horses knew where they were going, and all Henry and Martin had to do was stay on board.

Ginny guided them along a quiet track to the end of the stable's boundaries, through the sand dunes, and then Henry's breath caught in his throat when Missy set foot on the tropical beach. Palm trees lined the seashore, the soft sand was almost white, and Henry noticed pretty seashells dotted amongst the fine grains of sand. The far stretching Indian ocean had a turquoise tinge to it, but it was so clear that when Ginny guided them towards the gently lapping waves, he could see little fish merrily going about their fishy business. And somehow, seeing this view from horseback, through the two little brown ears in front of him, made it that much more magnificent. He was not on his own, he was sharing this moment with Missy, and he was starting to realise, just a little bit, why Sarah was so passionate about horses.

Sarah had been the reason behind his impulsive decision to come riding today. He wanted to step into her world and find out more about it for himself. And he also knew that being close to some horses would make him feel closer to Sarah.

"How are you guys doing?" called out Ginny. "Having fun?"

Henry was pleased to hear Martin reply, "Very much! Bessie is such a lovely horse."

"Yes, thank you," replied Henry.

"Let's go swimming!" announced Ginny, and she turned her docile horse towards the sea slowly encouraging him to take a dip. Missy and Bessy followed suit, and before Henry could say anything, the water was lapping around his waist and Missy's powerful legs were propelling them through the crystal-clear water. It was one of the most unbelievable and incredible sensations that Henry had every experienced. The trusting mare dutifully followed Ginny, right out of her depth, before swimming in a circle and turning back to shore until her strong hooves met the bed of sand, and she carefully carried Henry back to the water's edge. And the first thing Henry thought, when he was back on dry land, his clothes dripping wet, was, *I hope I get to tell Sarah!*

Ginny generously offered to take some pictures of them, on the sweet-tempered, perfectly well-behaved horses on the beautiful tropical beach, as a reminder of their first ever ride. Henry hoped that one day, he might be able to show them to Sarah.

Settled in the back of the air-conditioned taxi, Henry raised his eyebrows at Martin. "Well?"

"Ok, ok, I admit it, I had fun!" replied Martin with a hearty laugh.

"Good! Me too. Now we must get back to the grindstone!"

Henry climbed the six flights of stairs to his cabin with a spring in his step, feeling fully refreshed and ready to tackle his mountain of paperwork in preparation for setting sail tomorrow. As soon as he walked over to his desk, he saw it. A white envelope with 'air mail' stamped on it, and Sarah's familiar handwriting. His heart skipped a beat on seeing it. The much-anticipated letter had arrived.

Dear Henry,

I hope you are well, wherever you are! Things are crazy busy here for me at the moment and I'm enjoying every minute. My new boss is lovely, and the yard has twenty-nine horses, all of whom I adore. I'm starting to find my feet and so far, have enjoyed three exhilarating rides galloping across the beach with excited but experienced holiday makers.

My cottage is your typical picture-perfect Cornish cottage. The whole cottage is about the size of one of Barty and Caroline's stables! But I love it and it feels like home already.

I have enclosed my address so you can write back as soon as you have some free time.

Say hi to Martin from me and tell him that Kelly will be down to visit me soon.

Your friend,

Sarah

Henry read, then re-read his letter from Sarah, and feeling like he had just been swallowed up by a bubble of happiness, carefully folded it up, placed it inside the top drawer of his desk, then got to work.

Sarah

It was six o'clock in the morning, and as was her normal routine now, Sarah was sipping her morning cup of tea and munching through her plate of buttery toast. She had been in England for a month now, and although she was exhausted every night from all the physical work that came with working on a busy yard, she was the happiest she had ever been. She loved the day-to-day routine of the horses, and she loved the variety of the clients and the different types of holiday treks they wanted. She was also enjoying getting to know some of the locals for their weekly dressage lessons.

But today was going to be different. A few days ago, Tia had announced that just like the other girls who worked for her, Sarah also was allowed to keep her own horse at Elderberry. It was one of the perks of the job, she had said. And that little comment had planted a seed, and she hadn't been able to help herself. Each evening she had been scouring the horse for sale ads on the internet. Feeling so settled and knowing that she really was home made her think that it might be time to think about getting her own horse again. She knew that Gulliver was irreplaceable, but he was gone now, and she missed the friendship and the connection that she would have with her own horse. And then two days ago she had seen a picture, and something stirred within her. She didn't know what it was, but something was drawing her to the bright bay thoroughbred gelding. She had contacted the owner and had scheduled an appointment to meet him tomorrow on her day off. And to make the trip that much more exciting, Kelly would be arriving this evening. Sarah still did not have a car of her own so Kelly had generously offered to drive her to Devon to view the horse. They were going to have a relaxing meal together, catch each other up with all their gossip and tomorrow, they would meet the bright bay gelding.

Strolling along the country lane to work, in the weak morning sun, Sarah was beyond excited for her friend to arrive.

Sarah's day was hectic to say the least, but she was pleased as it kept her busy and focused until the last hay net was hung and final bucket of water filled, and her twenty-four hours of free time could finally start.

The pans on her little stove were bubbling away when she saw the headlights of Kelly's car as it pulled up into her driveway. Racing to her front door, she swung it open and met Kelly halfway down her crazy paved pathway to wrap her arms around her in a warm welcoming hug. It had been two and a half months since they had seen each other, and she had missed her greatly.

Settled on her squishy sofa with large bowls of spaghetti bolognaise on their laps, accompanied by a glass of wine, Sarah and Kelly chatted ten to the dozen about Kyle and Kelly's yard, Sarah's adventure at sea, the majestic Spanish horses, the lovely Martin, and the very dashing Captain Henry Hyam. Sarah had not had a girlfriend to share her thoughts and feelings with for nearly two decades, and she was now relishing her chance to divulge all her thoughts about the captain and the letters they had exchanged to her new confidante. They talked late into the night, and Kelly seemed as equally keen as she was about seeing what the future might hold for both her and Henry.

At eight o'clock the next morning, which both Sarah and Kelly agreed was most definitely a decent lie in, Sarah picked up the picnic bag and climbed into the passenger seat alongside Kelly.

"Ready?" grinned Kelly.

"Let's go," beamed Sarah.

The two hours flew by as they chatted, giggled, and sang their hearts out to the cheesy music blasting out of the car radio. Sarah was positively jigging in her seat when they finally turned into the driveway of the yard where the bay gelding was currently stabled. When Sarah got a feeling about a horse, she knew that the only thing she could do was follow her instincts whole-heartedly, and that was exactly what she was going to do today.

A middle-aged gentleman wearing battered denim jeans, a plaid work shirt and flat cap greeted them as they pulled up into the yard carpark.

"Sarah, I presume?" he asked as soon as the two women stepped out of the car.

"Hello, yes. You must be Jeremy? We spoke on the phone yesterday?" replied Sarah enthusiastically.

The man nodded as he shifted from foot to foot, seemingly unable to get his words out. "That's right," he eventually said.

Sarah and Kelly looked at each other, unsure about what to do next. Finally, Sarah took matters into her own hands and said, "Should we go and see the horse?"

Jeremy nodded again but didn't move. "The thing is, I'm not sure exactly what my wife told you when you enquired about him last week? She's actually away this weekend, gone to look at a new horse herself, that's why you got me for the directions."

"16 hand, four-year-old, bright bay, thoroughbred gelding," stated Sarah.

"That's right," agreed Jeremy. "Straight off the track. My wife has had quite a few ex-racers before, but never…er…quite like this one. Bit of a live wire, he is."

Unperturbed, Sarah suggested again that they go and view the horse. And this time, with seemingly nothing else to say, Jeremy led her towards the stable block where three horses poked their heads out of their respective stables in greeting.

"Here he is," said Jeremy, stopping outside of the first stable and pointing.

"What's his name? Your wife didn't actually tell me," admitted Sarah.

"Nicholas. His name is Nicholas."

Sarah walked right up to him and slowly offered him the back of her hand to sniff in greeting. As soon as she felt his delicate whispers touch her skin, she felt it. That indescribable pull, the desire to run her fingers through his silky black mane, the need to just be in his presence and the inner craving to soak in all of his beauty, because one thing was for sure, Nicholas was absolutely stunning.

"If you could tack him up and lead him into the school, I'd like to ride him please," announced Sarah.

Jeremy grimaced, offered a quick nod, then disappeared to get Nicholas' tack. A very uncomfortable few minutes commenced, for everyone involved, including Nicholas, whilst Jeremy manhandled the very uncooperative horse into his saddle and bridle. Jeremy then led the skittish horse out of his stable with Nicholas snorting and puffing as his iron shod hooves crashed around on the concrete yard sending sparks flying.

Sarah and Kelly looked at each other, slightly taken aback that Nicholas' true temperament had not been disclosed earlier.

"He's certainly something!" whispered Kelly.

But Sarah was still not discouraged. Her inner instincts had never failed her before, and she believed that they would not fail her now. She confidently followed Jeremy and Nicholas into the sand school took the end of his lead rope and relieved the very grateful Jeremy from the snorting, prancing horse.

"Hello, Nicholas," she whispered, and just like she had done the first time she met Persephone, she waited calmly and confidently. She did not know how many minutes had passed, but eventually her persistence paid off, and Nicholas began to settle. Tentatively holding out her hand she waited for Nicholas to meet her halfway, and in less than a minute he did. As soon as she felt his velvety soft muzzle snuffle her fingers, she felt a zing right through her body and tingles running through her veins. And when Nicholas slowly brought his head up, and looked right at her, she knew that he had felt it too. She slowly moved to his right-hand side and dropped the stirrup. Moving back to his head, she ran her fingers gently up his nose and scratched him under his forelock. Slowly moving to his left-hand side, she lowered the second stirrup. Smoothing his neck with her hands, she whispered, "Let's go riding."

In one smooth movement she swung herself up into his saddle. Nicholas exploded, as Sarah knew he would, and she was ready for it. She sat deep in his saddle, kept a light contact with the reins, and went with him. She asked him for nothing. She just sat there, calmly waiting. His bucking and squealing and bolting did not last long, and once he accepted Sarah as his rider, together they fluidly trotted around the school. Sarah felt like she was floating on air with his incredibly smooth gait and effortless changes of rein as they completed circles and serpentines around the school.

Nicholas seemed to be quite unfit, and he tired quickly after their schooling session, so Sarah brought him down to walk, patted him generously as they did two laps around the school to cool him down, and then they both ambled over to Kelly and Jeremy.

Beaming down at them both, she said to Jeremy, "I'll take him!"

Seemingly lost for words again, Jeremy just stared open mouthed back at her. "I've...he's...never before...I can't believe it," he stammered. Eventually, he managed to form a coherent sentence. "You can really ride. My wife hasn't even been able to get on him, let alone do what you just did. Incredible."

"So, I can buy him?"

"Yes, please! He's been nothing but a headache for us since he arrived three months ago. He's all yours."

"I hope you can put up with him for another two weeks?" enquired Sarah. "My friend said she could collect him for me with her horse box but she's flat out busy until Saturday after next. I can pay you now though."

Satisfied that he would be receiving payment for the problem horse in full, Jeremy reluctantly agreed to him staying for the two weeks. And after Jeremy agreed to Sarah's request that the horse was not to be put back in his stable, but to be turned out into one of the paddocks for the duration of his stay, Sarah untacked her new horse, kissed his nose and turned him out into the paddock.

Kelly had remained quiet whilst Sarah and Jeremy had been discussing Nicholas, and it wasn't until they were back in her car and bumbling back down the yards driveway that she finally spoke.

"I can't believe what you did with that horse Sarah. I mean, it looked like it had a serious screw loose, and then you got on it! The way you rode him, the way you communicated with him, and by the end of your ride he was behaving like a regular horse. You were just amazing to watch Sarah, you really were!" gushed her friend.

Blushing under her friend's shower of praise, Sarah simply said, "I just knew, as soon as I saw him, that he and I were meant to be together."

"I'm so pleased you have found your perfect horse, Sarah. And that I got to meet him!"

The rest of the car journey was spent discussing everything and anything regarding Nicholas, and after a quick pit stop at the local town's Chinese takeaway to pick up some supper, in no time at all, they were pulling into her driveway. Sarah was on cloud nine as she unlocked her door and stepped inside her cottage, the wafts of her dinner causing her stomach to growl in hunger, and then she saw it. There, sitting on her doormat was a white envelope with 'air mail' stamped on it and her name written in Henry's familiar handwriting. *Could this day get any better!*

Henry

Henry was standing on the bow of his ship under a clear blue sky and scorching sunshine. His eyes rested on the land mass ahead of him. After fourteen days of being at sea, he was anchored just offshore from Australia. In one hour's time his space in the dockyard would become available and he could then bring his ship into the Australian port of Sydney.

Enjoying the tranquillity of the calm ocean before him, he rested his arms on the ship's railings and breathed in the fresh salty sea air, and to his delight, a pod of dolphins chose that moment to break the surface and glide effortlessly through the water right before his eyes. They jumped and splashed and played, seeming to enjoy the fact that they had an eager spectator watching their gymnastic display. Henry recalled that the last time he had enjoyed such a show he'd had Sarah by his side to share the experience with him. The thought of her brought a smile to his lips, just as he had smiled when he stood back and watched her enjoy her first encounter with wild dolphins. He wondered what she was doing now, and if she had received his letter. He hoped that if he had timed the postal service correctly, and she was able to reply quickly, then there might just possibly be a letter waiting for him when he arrived in Sydney. He watched the dolphins elegantly glide away, and with anticipation fluttering through him, he made his way towards his bridge. He had lots of work to do before he would find out if there was a letter waiting for him.

Henry and Martin had been to Australia many times, and it had now become a little tradition of theirs to frequent a small but atmospheric pub situated in walking distance from the docks. Sitting in the beer garden, enjoying the view of Sydney harbour, Henry and Martin sipped their ice-cold beers before tucking into their generous portions of steak pie and chips.

"Ahhh, it's good to be back," said Martin. "Nothing beats Australia! And we have a whole week to enjoy it before we head back to Thailand!"

Henry smiled at his friend. He knew how much Martin loved Australia - he had even lived in a little town just outside of Sydney for a few years when he was in his twenties. He had spent every moment of his leave travelling all over the country in his bashed up pick-up truck, and Henry always enjoyed the stories he told of his outback adventures. But although Henry was enjoying his downtime with his friend, he could not give him his full concentration because at the back of his mind he was thinking of Sarah. He was anxious to know if a letter would be waiting for him when he returned to the ship.

"I was thinking of hiring a car and taking a drive up to the Blue Mountains, maybe even stay the night," continued Martin. "Want to join me?"

Henry mulled over the idea whilst taking a refreshing swig of his beer. *A trip out with Martin might actually be a good distraction,* thought Henry. A solitary week in his cabin was perhaps not the most useful way of spending his week off.

"Cheer up!" said Martin. "I'm sure you'll hear from her soon!"

"What?" stuttered Henry. "Hear from who?"

Martin raised his eyes at him in that knowing way of his. "Sarah, of course! It's obvious you're waiting on a letter from her. I saw how you looked at each other at Barty's, and I saw the letter you got in Thailand with the British air mail stamp!"

Henry was not particularly surprised that Martin had put all of the pieces together by himself. He was astute like that. Good at reading people and even better at correctly filling in the gaps with his own intuition.

"Ok," admitted Henry, "you're right. Sarah and I have been writing to each other!"

"I knew it! Come on then, drink up. Let's go back to the ship and see if anything has arrived. I won't get any sense out of you until you find out! And then we'll plan our trip, agreed?"

"Agreed!" replied Henry. He was pleased to have the whole situation with Sarah out in the open with his friend, and equally pleased that he hadn't had to say anything about it all!

The two friends chatted easily as they strolled back to the dockyard, and just as they climbed over the gangplank and set foot on deck, the second mate came bustling over to them.

"Chief, a message has just come in for you," he announced, handing over a folded piece of paper.

Thanking the second mate, Martin turned to Henry, "Go on! Go and see if it's arrived. I'll deal with this and catch up with you later." Henry watched his chief purposely march away to his own cabin.

And there it was. The much-awaited letter had been placed by his steward on top of his paperwork on his desk. Henry grinned down at it, picked it up and ran his fingers across his name written in Sarah's hand.

Dear Henry

Thank you so much for the postcard and letter from Thailand. I can't tell you how thrilled I was to hear of your very first horse ride, and on a tropical Thai beach no less! And you have even done something with horses that I have never done... swimming! I hope it was the most wonderful experience for you.

Well today has been one of the best days of my life and I couldn't wait to tell you about it. Kelly and I went to view a horse. He's an ex-race horse, who's given himself a bit of a name for being a trouble maker! But I have to tell you, in my opinion, I think he is absolutely perfect in every way. And he's going to be mine! I bought him straight away. Unfortunately, I have two very long weeks ahead of me until my boss is available to collect him for me with her horse box, but no doubt I will be kept busy at work, so fingers crossed the time passes quickly. I've already been shown which stable is to be his, he'll be right next door to Gwendoline, the yard's mischievous miniature Shetland. I have a feeling Nicholas and Gwendoline are going to get along like a house on fire!

Maybe one day you will get to meet him.

I look forward to hearing from you soon, and I hope that you are enjoying Australia (have you even arrived yet? I have no idea how long it will take you to sail there from Thailand!)

From your friend

Sarah

Henry enjoyed the feelings of positivity that oozed out of Sarah's newsy letter and the fact that she seemed so happy and settled. And did he detect a possible invitation to visit her in Cornwall? The words, 'maybe one day you will get to meet him' stared back at him from the paper, and the idea of potentially visiting Sarah when he was next on leave swirled around his mind. He could think of nothing that he would like more than to be in the company of his enchanting Sarah. He looked at the date at the top of the letter. It was dated exactly two weeks ago. He smiled to himself. Nicholas would be arriving today! And the thought of how excited Sarah must be, right in this very moment, made him feel a closeness to her despite the thousands of miles between them.

He was still holding the letter in his hands when Martin arrived at his door. "It's here!" he said waving the letter. "Now let's get to planning our trip to the mountains!"

Martin didn't reply. In fact, on closer inspection, Henry realised his friend was looking rather pale. "Is everything ok?" he asked.

"Captain, Henry, I have some bad news. I think maybe we should both sit down."

Henry sat back down in his chair at his desk and gestured for Martin to take the comfy chair opposite him. Henry cleared his mind and tried to mentally prepare himself for whatever his friend had to tell him.

"Work?" he enquired, his first thought for what the problem might be.

He watched Martin shake his head. "I've just got off the phone from Kyle. Sarah's in hospital."

"What?" blurted out Henry, struggling to process what he had just heard, all the while thinking that it couldn't possibly be true. Sarah was getting her new horse today. How could she possibly be in hospital? It didn't make any sense.

"Our Sarah?" he asked, desperately trying to clarify the situation, but deep down knowing that both he and Martin did not know another Sarah.

Martin nodded. "Kelly drove straight down to Cornwall this morning, she's with her now."

"But what happened? Has she had a riding accident? Did something happen with her new horse?" Henry's mind was spinning with questions, and he felt frustration flood through him at being so far away from her.

"No," Martin said carefully, "nothing to do with horses. That was the first thing I asked, but Kyle didn't go into any more detail than that. But," he stammered, "but he said she's in a really bad way, and that he would know more once Kelly had spoken to the doctors. Apparently, she put Kelly down as her next of kin for her new job so at least the doctors will be able to explain everything about Sarah's condition and prognosis to her."

Henry was in shock. How could he go from feeling complete elation to utter devastation in the space of two minutes? Henry sat in silence whilst he carefully processed what Martin had told him, and slowly a plan began to form in his mind.

"I'm going to call Barty," he told Martin. Martin started to raise himself out of the chair to no doubt give him some privacy, but Henry didn't want that. He needed Martin to hear what Barty had to say and he gestured for Martin to stay exactly where he was.

His phone call to Barty lasted no longer than five minutes. He did not waste time with small talk. Instead, he shared all the information he had about Sarah as soon as Barty answered his phone. And Barty handled the situation immediately. He ordered Henry to get to the airport straight away. A flight ticket to England would be organised for him by the time he arrived. Barty insisted that he must go to Sarah – his upcoming week's leave would be spent in Cornwall. He would have time to visit Sarah and be back in Australia in time to set sail to Thailand. And he was to contact Barty with news of Sarah's condition as soon as he could.

Sarah

Sarah's head felt fuzzy. It was as if a thick fog had entered her mind and she couldn't quite see through the mist. It was proving tricky to open her eyes, and her body felt so terribly heavy. She tried to focus. She could hear a bleeping noise in the distance. *That must be my alarm,* she thought. She tried to lift her hand. She wanted to find her phone so she could switch it off, but all she could manage was a weak fumble.

"Nurse," she heard. "Nurse, come quickly, I think she's waking up," continued the mysterious voice.

"Sarah, can you hear me?" asked a second unfamiliar voice.

She tried to sit up. Something definitely wasn't right, but she couldn't quite put her finger on it.

"Sarah, can you hear me?" the voice asked again.

She tried to reply but all she could muster up was a gurgling grunt, and it was all feeling like quite a lot of effort to wake up right now. Perhaps she should go back to sleep for a little while longer.

"Sarah, it's me, Kelly." Sarah felt a warm hand clasp around her own.

What on earth is Kelly doing here? she wondered to herself. With incredible effort, she managed to lift her heavy lids and to her astonishment, she saw Kelly's big brown eyes staring down at her.

"Nurse," she heard Kelly call out. "She's awake."

A moment later, a lady in a blue nurse's uniform was standing over her. "Hello, Sarah. You're going to be ok, love. You're in the hospital. Your friend Kelly is here with you. I'm going to go and fetch the doctor."

Two hours later, heavily drugged up on pain killers, Sarah was sitting up in her hospital bed trying to understand that it was not actually Friday evening, but Sunday afternoon. She quietly listened to Kelly explain about how she had got there.

"Tia found you on Saturday morning. After you didn't show up on time for work, she went to your cottage to see if she could find you. She said that your front door was open, and she saw you as soon as she stepped inside. You were unconscious, Sarah. She called the ambulance straight away, and then once they had taken you off to hospital, she called the police. She thought it very unusual that your door was open. The doctors have alerted the police that you have woken up, they'll be here in about an hour to ask you questions. What happened, Sarah? Can you remember?" asked Kelly.

Sarah was trying to take in all the information that Kelly had just given her, and slowly, very slowly it began to dawn on her that she did in fact remember. Just as she was trying to form the words to explain everything to Kelly, there was a knock on her hospital door. The friendly nurse who had been with her when she first woke up popped her head around the door.

"A visitor has arrived for you. Would you like me to send him in?"

Sarah and Kelly looked at each other, both wondering who it could possibly be. Kelly took hold of her hand and gently squeezed it. Sarah appreciated her comforting gesture, then curious to find out who it was, replied to the nurse, "Ok, send him in."

"Henry!" gasped Sarah, "what on earth are you doing here?"

She watched him hover in the doorway, and she noticed a flicker of concern and shock pass over his eyes before he composed himself and offered her one of his warm smiles.

"Kyle told Martin that you had been admitted to hospital," explained Henry.

"And both Barty and I agreed that I should come and see you. So," he said tentatively, "here I am."

Sarah couldn't quite believe that the captain was standing right in front of her, and with the way her head was thumping, and her body was aching, she privately dreaded what she must look like to him. And deep in the pit of her stomach, she felt a knotted ball of anxiety beginning to form at the thought of trying to work out how exactly she was going to explain to him how she had ended up in hospital.

"It's so lovely to see you," was all she could think of to say to him.

"Hi, I'm Kelly," said Kelly, breaking through the awkward silence. Sarah watched her get up, shake Henry's hand, then pull over another seat. "Kyle told me you have flown all the way from Australia. You must be exhausted, take a seat."

Just as Henry sat down beside her, and her whizzing mind was trying to come up with the right thing to say, there came another knock on the door. This time two police officers came into her room, introduced themselves and announced they were there to take her statement about Friday night. Before Henry and Kelly had a chance to get up and leave, she spoke up. "I'd like them to stay please," she told the officers. The police officers agreed, and when everyone was quiet around her, she started with, "I know who did this to me. It was my husband, Julian."

She didn't dare look at Henry. Instead, she focused on the officers scribbling away in their notebooks.

"And has this sort of thing happened to you before in your marriage?" one of them asked.

"Yes, regularly over the past nineteen years." She looked at Kelly for reassurance that she was doing the right thing by finally voicing what Julian had done to her. Kelly's subtle nod assured her that she was.

"Talk us through what happened on Friday night, Sarah," said the other officer.

Taking a deep breath, she mustered up as much courage that she could find within her to enable her to relive the night that Julian nearly killed her.

"I was at home. It was late, about nine o'clock, I think. I was sitting on my sofa eating dinner when I heard a knock at the door." Her blood ran cold, just like it had done when she opened the door and saw Julian standing right in front of her.

"I was so shocked to see him that I was rooted to the spot. By the time I had regained the use of my legs, he had already come into my house and closed the door. He locked it, then slipped the key into his pocket." She remembered the feeling of claustrophobia engulfing her as she realised there was no way out for her.

"He only talked to begin with. He wanted to know where I had been and how I had manged to get by without any money. And how I had ended up in Cornwall. I told him I'd been working for Kelly's brother-in-law for a while and then moved to Cornwall as soon as I got offered the job here. I tried to keep my replies as simple as possible. I didn't want to give him even more of an excuse to….. Well, to do this," and she shrugged, knowing that everyone knew exactly what she meant.

"And then he picked me up and threw me against the locked door, and before I fell to the ground, he caught me and slammed me so hard against the door again I could feel my own warm blood trickling down the back of my neck." She could also remember the pain searing through her head and his malicious, steely eyes staring at her.

"By this point he was really angry. I think all of his pent-up frustration about what I'd done just came spiralling out of him. He punched me square in the face, and once I had fallen to the floor, he kicked me over and over again. And the next thing I remember is waking up here," she concluded.

She still could not look at Henry. *What must he think of me?* But she knew she had done the right thing by asking him to stay. He deserved to know the truth.

"Just to confirm for our records," said an officer, breaking through her thoughts. "The doctor's report states that you have suffered broken ribs, a sprained wrist, a head wound that needed stiches and that you were physically beaten to the point of unconsciousness by your husband. Is that correct, Sarah?"

"Yes, that's correct."

"We will be in contact as soon as your husband has been located. Thank you for your statement, and goodbye Sarah."

After the officers left, there was a heavy atmosphere in her room. She knew that Kelly was struggling to process just how abusive Julian had actually been towards her. And she couldn't even hazard a guess at what Henry might be thinking about the whole sorry situation. The three of them were quiet for a short while, no one really knowing how to proceed after hearing Sarah's harrowing ordeal.

Eventually, Kelly's voice rang out in the silent, stuffy air. "Tia told me that Nicholas seems to be settling in well."

Pleased with hearing news of her horse, and relieved with the distraction, Sarah replied, "Tia went and collected him on her own for me?"

"We both agreed that it was pointless us both waiting here with you when the doctors had informed us that you were very unlikely to wake up on Saturday, and we both believed that it was what you would want her to do. Although," she continued, with a smile on her lips, "I think Nicholas reserves his best behaviour only for you at the moment. I hear he has been quite the character on the yard! He's out in the paddock with Gwendoline, I believe Tia thinks they have met each other's match! Tia said she'd pop in and see you tomorrow, you can ask her all about him then."

Sarah physically felt herself relax on hearing her beautiful boy was in his new home, waiting for her. Kelly got up, acutely aware that Sarah and Henry had much to talk about. "I'd better give Kyle a quick ring, he'll be wanting to know how you are." She cast a warm look at both Sarah and Henry, then quietly left the room.

Sarah couldn't put it off any longer. She slowly and painfully shifted herself so that she could look directly at Henry.

"What must you think of me?" she asked, then without waiting for a reply, she ploughed on. "I'm so very sorry, Henry. I never meant to keep Julian a secret from you, it's just," she stammered, "it's just that I wanted to block him out. I didn't want to think about him. I didn't want his darkness contaminating the freedom I felt when I was on your ship." She looked away from him as she felt colour rushing to her cheeks. "And I was embarrassed," she admitted.

She felt Henry gently rest his fingers under her jaw line, and slowly lift her chin until she was looking directly at him again.

"Sarah, you have absolutely nothing to apologise for, and you certainly shouldn't feel any sort of embarrassment for what that brute has done to you. I completely understand you not wishing to share this with me, honestly, I do. I only you wish you had told me so that I could help you. You do know that I would do anything for you Sarah, don't you?"

Sarah could see his heartfelt emotion through his bright blue eyes staring back at her, and she knew he was telling the truth. She knew that he was her friend, and that she could trust him. She nodded solemnly to show that she understood, and then she watched Henry slowly rise out his chair and lean over. Then he tenderly kissed her forehead.

Henry

Henry visited Sarah at the hospital over the next two days until the doctors deemed her ready to go home, and he was hugely relieved to hear her news that Julian had now been located and was in police custody. He would no longer be a threat to Sarah when she left the hospital. It transpired that Julian had been watching Kelly and Kyle for weeks in the hope of finding his wife. And it was the change in Kelly's routine that had encouraged him to follow her the day she left to visit Sarah in Cornwall, and unknowingly to her, she had led him right to Sarah's front door. He had bided his time until he knew Sarah would be home from work and all alone in her little cottage, powerless to escape him.

Sarah was not to go back to work for at least a week, and then after that it was only to teach from the ground. Her broken ribs needed time to heal, and the heavy physical side of her work would have to be put on hold for at least a month. She was also told she was not to ride because if she were to fall, she would damage her already heavily abused body.

Kelly had left, with the promise of coming back down to Cornwall soon. Unfortunately, the horses did not look after themselves! And she couldn't leave Kyle to manage everything on his own for too long. Henry had assured her that Sarah would be in his very capable hands, and that he would look after her for the duration of his stay.

Henry had organised a taxi to take them both back to Sarah's house. He was keen to see her settled before his car picked up him up in a few hours' time to take him back to the airport.

"All ready?" he asked Sarah.

Taking hold of his arm to steady herself, she grinned up at him. "As ready as I'll ever be."

They chatted amongst themselves during the half an hour drive from the hospital to Sarah's home. When the car turned into the country lane with a big signpost saying, 'Elderberry Stables," he saw Sarah sit up in anticipation.

"Would it be ok if we popped into the yard first? Only for a couple of minutes. I'm just dying to see Nicholas!"

Even though the doctor had explicitly expressed she was to go straight home and rest, Henry knew that she would never be able to settle until she had seen her new horse, and it would be futile to try and stop her. Henry asked the driver to pull into the yard and wait for them, assuring him that they would not be long. He watched Sarah inelegantly haul her aching body out of the taxi before the driver had even turned the ignition off. Henry offered her his arm, secretly enjoying being able to have a reason to be useful, and he couldn't deny that he also liked the feeling of her resting against him, and together, they walked over to Nicholas' paddock.

"Isn't he just beautiful," gushed Sarah, before calling out his name.

Henry watched the magnificent horse stand to attention. As soon as he heard Sarah's voice, he held his head up high, his body poised and alert, and his ears pricked as he focused only on her. She called him again, and as if an explosion had gone off, he burst into action, covering the ground between them in moments, and then Henry heard a sound he had never heard a horse make before. And he realised that Nicholas was making the sound only for Sarah. He assumed it could only be an intimate gesture, and no doubt one that Sarah understood. As she whispered into his ears, and ran her hands over his nose, the horse nuzzled her affectionately. But when Henry put his hand out to greet the horse, Nicholas pulled back sharply to avoid his touch.

"Don't mind him," Sarah laughed. "He's not really a people person! He'll settle down soon, I'm sure of it. It's just going to take some time for him to learn how to trust people. Racehorses are bred for one thing," she explained, "and that's to race! And it can take time for them to adjust to the outside world."

Henry could see that Nicholas only had eyes for his new mistress, and it pleased him that he would be leaving Sarah in the care of such a loyal friend.

"But she'll let you pet her!" announced Sarah.

"Who?" questioned Henry. And then he felt a nudge against his shin and looked down to find the tiniest pony he had ever seen.

"Gwendoline!" announced Sarah. "Bit of a bossy boots she is, and pretty demanding for affection and treats from anyone who comes on her yard!"

Whilst dutifully petting the adorable Gwendoline, Henry realised that he was beginning to understand how very different each individual horse was. They all had their own quirks and personal identities, and Sarah seemed to instinctively know just how to interact with each of them. He could also understand why Sarah was so very happy in her new job. He could see horses every which way he looked - in the paddocks, in the stables, and off in the distance he could see a string of them plodding sedately across the open beach. She was completely submerged in a world of horses and living her dream life. *Horses to Sarah are just like the sea to me,* he mused, understanding the depths of her passion. And now she had Nicholas. Henry stood up from his crouched position of petting Gwendoline, and he watched Sarah and Nicholas in their private world consisting of just the two of them. Nicholas was resting his regal head on Sarah's shoulder, listening intently to her secret whispers. The scene unfolding before his eyes left Henry wondering, hoping, if Sarah might ever feel the same way about him?

Henry would have liked to quietly watch Sarah and her horse for hours, but following the doctors' orders, he tentatively suggested to Sarah that she should say goodbye. He assured her that Nicholas was in good hands with both Tia and Gwendoline; it was time for Sarah to go home.

Sarah welcomed Henry into her very homely cottage, and Henry made a mental note to quickly memorise as many of the little details as possible. When he was far away from her, in the middle of the ocean, he would be able to picture her curled up on the sofa fully engrossed in one of her books, pottering away in her kitchen, or with Nicholas, at the yard. Once she was settled comfortably on the sofa, Henry made them both a cup a tea and sliced up the delicious homemade Victoria sponge cake Tia had left in Sarah's kitchen to welcome her home.

Henry delved into his suitcase and produced a parcel for Sarah. Handing it over to her, he said, "I'm afraid there wasn't much choice in the hospital gift shop, but I think this might be something you'll enjoy, and hopefully keep you entertained whilst you are off work." He watched Sarah eagerly open up the parcel, and saw delight spread across her face as she pulled out her new book.

"*All Creatures Great and Small* by James Herriot!" she squealed. "I've never read this one before, I can't wait to get started. Thank you so much Henry." Then to Henry's surprise, she leaned forward and planted a kiss on his cheek.

"I thought we could read the first chapter together," said Henry, carefully taking the book out of her hands. Reading to Sarah, all those weeks ago, when she was so very poorly with seasickness, had been lodged in Henry's memory forever. He had found it a thoroughly enjoyable experience sharing a book with someone who was as equally enthralled by it as he was. And Sarah's love of books was one of the many reasons he was falling in love with her.

Henry and Sarah lost themselves in the Yorkshire dales and the day-to-day life of a busy vet, both chuckling out loud at the antics some of his animal patients got up to! Henry continued to read, at Sarah's insistence, up until half-way through chapter three, and after what felt like no time at all, he heard the sound of his airport transfer car pull up onto Sarah's driveway.

"I must go," he announced as he carefully placed the book down on the sofa and stood up. Without saying a word, he held out his arm when Sarah indicated that she would also like to get up. He felt her weight on his arm as she slowly eased herself off the sofa, and then she was in his arms. After months of dreaming about what it might feel like to hold her, now he could feel her slight frame leaning against his body for support, and he could smell her familiar intoxicating citrus scent. He held her as tightly as he dared, fearing that if he wrapped his arms around her too tightly, he might hurt her bruised body and broken ribs. A flash of anger surged through him at what her husband had done to her. He just couldn't understand what might possess any man to treat another human being so brutally. He could not fathom what must have gone through that man's head in order for him to lash out so violently, over and over again.

He felt her pull away from him, and she slowly looked up into his eyes. He could feel his heart pounding beneath his shirt as he lowered his head and gently brushed his lips over hers.

"I'll be on leave in five weeks," he told her.

"Nicholas and I will be waiting," she assured him.

Reluctantly, he released his arms from around her and for the first time ever, he had a momentary thought that he did not want to go back to work. He did not want to walk out of her little cottage and leave her behind. But it was only fleeting. He knew, deep down, that even though he loved Sarah with every fibre in his body, he could not turn his back on his life at sea. He was a captain of the sea, and it was she who was the alluring mistress of his soul.

Henry climbed into the car, and as it trundled down the country road, he kept his eyes only on Sarah, waving to him, until she was just a tiny speck in the distance. *Five weeks,* he thought, *that really is no time at all, and then she will be back in my arms.* With the thought of holding Sarah in his arms again, he felt the familiar draw inside him. He was going back to sea. Back to his beloved ship, his crew and his work. *But this time, Sarah will be waiting for me.* The long weeks of his leave would be filled with Sarah, and he wondered, just wondered, if it was possible for him to have them both? Would Sarah's intense passion for her horses enable her to understand his own passion for the sea? Or was he just fooling himself? Would Sarah be able to accept the many months he would be away from her? Did she really understand the life he led? The questions swirled around his mind as the car sped mile after mile on the motorway. All he could do was hope that Sarah understood him for who he truly was.

Sarah

Sarah was sitting on her sofa, sipping her morning cup of tea, staring at the envelope in front of her. She knew what it was. Her solicitor had contacted her two days ago to inform her that the paperwork was on its way. She took a deep breath, then tore open the envelope, and with shaking hands, she saw it, right there in front of her in black and white. Julian had been charged with grievous bodily harm. As well as her own very damning statement, Kelly had readily agreed to tell the police everything she knew about what Julian had done to Sarah. The police also found Julian's DNA on Sarah's blood-stained clothes as well as a receipt in his car from the local Cornish garage for a full tank of fuel and a coffee, proving him to be in the area on the night of the attack.

Sarah couldn't quite believe it. She was finally free, and her toxic marriage would very soon be coming to an end. The courts had agreed whole heartedly with her request for a divorce and through numerous discussions between their lawyers, Julian had agreed to a swift divorce, and with it, a generous financial settlement. Julian had already signed the paperwork, and any day now, the papers would arrive for her own signature. Once signed, she would no longer be a married woman.

She sat quietly, hardly daring to believe that her nineteen years of fear and abuse had finally come to an end. And she felt an unfamiliar feeling surge through her. *Is that pride?* she mused. She thought about how her life had changed unrecognisably over the last few months and she knew, deep down, that it was because she, Sarah, had dug deep and found the strength to leave her abusive husband and start again, all on her own. Her new, wonderful friends had helped her in every way that they could, but it was Sarah who had actually found the gumption to do it. She felt tears trickling down her face as her thoughts turned to Gulliver, her beautiful, darling Gulliver. She owed him everything and she would forever be grateful for his constant loyalty and his friendship that never wavered.

A loud bang on her door brought her away from her thoughts.

"Sarah, are you ready?" called out Tia through the closed door. "It's time to go, we don't want to be late!"

Sarah jumped up, eager to greet Tia who was taking her to see the doctor for her check-up. She would hopefully be told that she was now allowed to ride again.

Sitting in the doctor's office, Tia asked for the third time, "And you're absolutely sure?"

Sarah laughed at Tia for her persistence, but deep down she was grateful that her boss, her friend, was looking out for her well-being with such dedication.

"Yes," replied the doctor. "Sarah can now take on light duties again at work and she can get back to riding horses."

"Well, I suppose I could let her start taking out some beginner hacks." Tia turned to Sarah. "Walking only, mind. You heard the doctor, light duties only."

Sarah couldn't help but catch the doctor's eye, and giving him a broad grin, she replied to Tia, "Ok, Ok, I concede, walking hacks only for the first few days. Can I get back to work now please?"

"Thank you, doctor," said Tia, and as she ushered Sarah out of his office. "Tomorrow you can take the morning walk, just for a hack around the lanes, and then we'll take it from there."

Tia pulled up on the yard. Sarah's plan was to head straight back to work, but Tia had firmly announced that she was not booked in to teach any dressage lessons that day, and riding was not to start until tomorrow. Therefore, Sarah had a long afternoon ahead of her, and she intended to spend it with Nicholas. With little work to keep her occupied over the previous four weeks, Sarah had dedicated all her time to Nicholas. The equine dentist, vet, farrier, and saddler had all been out to see him and declared him to be in ship shape condition to start his new career as her riding horse.

The huge amount of money that Barty had deposited into her bank account for her work at sea had barely been touched since she arrived in Cornwall. Her monthly rent was deducted from her wages, and what was left had been more than enough for her to live on, so Nicholas has been given the best of everything. She was dying to try out his brand-new black leather, general purpose saddle and equally beautiful black leather bridle. She had also treated herself to some new riding clothes. Apart from the small bag that Kyle retrieved from Julian's house on her behalf, she'd had nothing. She and Tia had enjoyed a lovely day out shopping for riding clothes, then followed it up with a delicious Cornish cream tea at a little boutique café on the way home.

Her days had been spent free schooling Nicholas in the sand school and walking him in hand around the quiet country lanes and down to the beach to familiarise him with his new surroundings. She was thrilled that he was slowly but surely becoming a calm and sensible horse. He also very much enjoyed the company of the other horses and could be turned out with any of the other twenty-nine horses on the yard. He wasn't aggressive or bossy towards them and seemed to relish the new sociable life he was living. This gave Sarah confidence that if he proved to be as safe as she hoped he would be after their ride today, he would become her lead horse for escorting the country lane and beach hacks. She was positively buzzing with excitement to find out just how fast he could run when she let him loose on the wide-open beach.

"Hello boy," she whispered to her horse when he greeted her at his paddock gateway. "Shall we go riding today?" And he nuzzled her neck and snuffled her hair in response. Sarah groomed him until he shone, tacked him up, then stood back to admire him in all of his glory. He really was the most magnificent specimen of a horse, and by far the most beautiful of all the horses on the yard. Sarah glowed from the inside out knowing that the gorgeous gelding standing before her was hers.

She led him into the sand school, put her foot in the stirrup and swung into his saddle. Nicholas didn't move a muscle. He just casually stood there, cool as a cucumber, giving every impression that this is how they always did things. In no way did he imply, *or admit,* Sarah thought, giggling to herself, that bucking, bolting, and squealing had ever been on the cards. "Ok," Sarah whispered to the horse. "We'll pretend our first meeting never happened! And if you behave today, I will forever call you the perfect gentleman!" And she giggled again as Nicholas twitched his ears in response.

Sarah and Nicholas walked, trotted, and cantered effortlessly around the school; his behaviour was so impeccable that after half an hour she decided that he was perfectly safe to take for a little plod down to the beach.

It was a calm day, and although there was a chill in the fresh sea air, the sun was shining brightly down on them as they plodded along the quiet beach. Sarah looked far out to sea and thought of Henry. She would never forget the loyalty and kindness he had shown her by flying all the way to England to be with her during her time of need. He had left his ship, and she knew that the decision to do so would not have been taken lightly. She wondered where he was in the world right now. And she hoped that he was just as contended with his life as she was, right in that very moment. He was on his ship, and she was with her horse. She pictured him on his bridge, sipping his coffee, far away in the middle of the ocean, in his happy place. And she presumed the same feelings must swirl through his veins, just like they did hers when she was in the company of horses. If anyone were to understand her deep rooted passion for horses, it was Henry. Wonderful, generous-hearted Henry. Her captain. And she would be seeing him next week! Excitement and happiness had bubbled out of her when Henry informed her that he had hired a little holiday cottage in the neighbouring village to the stables for his leave. "Henry's coming to Cornwall," she excitedly squealed to her horse. And she wondered if Henry thought about her as much as she thought about him.

Sarah had two options now. She could either follow the path through the sand dunes and head back to the yard along the country lanes, or she could turn around and find out how well behaved the new and improved Nicholas was and exactly how fast her boy could run.

She schooled him first. Alone on the wide-open beach, she and Nicholas walked, trotted, and cantered, just like they had done in the school at the beginning of their ride. He followed her instructions eagerly and when asked to transition down a gait, his brakes seemed to be in full working order. She trotted him purposefully in one final circle, pointed towards home, and asked for canter. His ears were pricked as he quickened his pace to a steady, rocking horse canter. She gave him a little squeeze with her legs, and he willingly picked up his pace to a fast canter.

Sarah could feel the fresh breeze whipping around her hair and complete, utter elation filled her soul as she and Nicholas powered across the beach. And then she asked him for his fifth gear. She had never ridden a racehorse before, and no previous riding experience prepared her for the immense surge in speed that Nicholas reached when he opened up into full gallop. They flew over the sand with Nicholas' thundering hooves eating up the ground before him.

Breathing heavily, Sarah asked Nicholas to slow down. They were nearing the track that would lead them home. Snorting and prancing after his exhilarating run, Nicholas settled himself and reverted back to his riding school pony style plod, and together, they ambled back to the yard.

"I thought we'd agreed walking only, Sarah!" called out Tia as soon as she arrived on the yard.

With a guilty tinge to her voice, she stammered, "Um, well, you see, the thing is…"

Tia burst out laughing. "I saw you and Nicholas blasting across the beach like you were in your own private race! Blimey that horse is fast. My poor horses won't have a chance at keeping up with him on the beach rides," she chuckled. "So, I guess you're back to work properly then?"

"Yes, absolutely! Thank you, Tia," gushed Sarah.

Sarah dismounted Nicholas, and with a spring in her step, she led him back to his stable and untacked him. After grooming him down, she wrapped her arms around him and hugged him tightly, then she held his face in her hands and planted a kiss on his velvety soft nose. "You're my best friend," she whispered to him. "Thank you for just being you." And, as she inhaled his intoxicating sweet horsey smell, she knew that whatever life threw in her way, she and Nicholas would face it together. Neither of them were alone anymore, they had each other. And they would be together every single day. Sometimes she couldn't quite believe her own luck. Her job was literally to hang out with her best friend every day. Nicholas would be her lead horse and idling along the country lanes and galloping across the beach was how they would be spending their days. And she would be paid for it! She wouldn't wish to change her life for anything in the world. She was without a doubt living her best life.

Henry

Henry and Martin were sitting in his cabin, sipping cold coca colas, chatting contentedly between themselves. The second mate was on watch, and tomorrow, Henry would be bringing his ship into the South African port of Cape Town. And after that, he would finally be seeing Sarah again. She was never far from his thoughts, and since they had exchanged phone numbers when they saw each other in Cornwall the previous month, he had not had to suffer the long weeks wait before her letters would arrive. They had been communicating almost daily.

"How will you spend your leave?" enquired Martin. "Any plans?"

Although Martin was aware that Sarah was now a dear friend to him and very much in the picture, he had not asked for any more information on the matter. And Henry was yet to disclose his plans to spend his leave with her.

"What are you doing?" he replied, deliberately stalling for time so he could best decide how to tell Martin.

"I'm off to Kyle and Kelly's for a while. My house is rented out, so they've offered for me to use their place as a base."

"I'm spending my first night's leave with Caroline and Barty. Caroline insisted apparently!" laughed Henry. "And then," he continued, "well, I'm going to Cornwall."

"To see Sarah, I presume?" replied Martin, a warm smile on his face.

And the cat was well and truly out of the bag. "Yes," he replied honestly.

Then Martin and Henry did something that they had never done before. They talked, really talked, about their lives away from sea. And they talked about women. How difficult they had both found it to maintain a relationship with the jobs they held. The distance was so hard for the woman at home, not understanding their passion to live a life at sea, their need to travel all over the world. And they questioned if they could ever see themselves settling down. And Henry confided that he and Sarah were slowly becoming more than friends and his concerns that the very different lives they led might be too much for a relationship to bear.

During his quiet moments, usually when he was on watch late at night, Henry had found himself mulling over the idea of living a life on the land. He asked himself whether he could give up the sea for Sarah, and there had been moments when he thought he could. He felt that if Sarah were to ask the question when they were together in Cornwall, he would like to know what his answer might be, but at the moment, he really didn't know. Which in itself was somewhat surprising. The fact that he was even seriously considering it proved to him how much he loved Sarah and how he desperately wanted to share his life with her.

"Would you give it up?" asked Henry.

Martin was quiet for a while, and Henry waited patiently for him to carefully consider his answer.

"I think that if I met the right woman, then I might. I think that the decision would have to be mine, though. I would probably resent her if she just outright asked me to leave my life and the sea for her. But if over time, I came to the decision myself because I wanted to marry her and spend the rest of my life with her, and I thought that would be best for both of us, then I think I would definitely consider it."

Henry listened intently as Martin voiced everything Henry had been thinking himself.

Then Martin continued, "I think you will probably have a good idea of what you want to do after your leave in Cornwall."

"I hope so," Henry replied quietly.

Henry and Martin's heartfelt conversation came to an end when Martin announced it was time for him to relieve the second mate, leaving Henry alone with his thoughts.

Barty arrived in his cabin two hours after his ship was docked in the port of Cape Town. He was his usual eccentric self and successfully bustled his way through Henry's somewhat sombre mood about his decision making and allowed him to relax and welcome the fun night ahead of him.

His cabin was clean and tidy, ready for the next captain to take over whilst he was on leave for three months, and with his two cases in his hands, he followed the exuberant Barty down the six flights of stairs, across the gangplank and onto South African land.

Barty stopped next to his gleaming navy-blue Aston Martin. "She drives like an absolute dream!" he announced, fondly stroking the car's bonnet. "I am driving you home myself!" Popping open the boot for Henry to store his luggage in, Barty jumped into the driver's seat. "Chop chop, we mustn't keep Caroline waiting!"

Henry had forgotten just how enjoyable Barty's company was and he felt very grateful that Caroline insisted he join them this evening. He knew he would now be leaving South Africa with a much more positive mindset regarding his future with Sarah than if he had stepped straight off his ship and onto a plane.

True to form, Caroline and Barty were in excellent spirits and were welcoming hosts, as always. Barty busied himself at his bar, keen to show off his new cocktail concoction, complete with cherries on sticks and flecks of edible gold sprinkled on top. And Caroline was keen to discuss Sarah. They were in regular contact, and she just couldn't believe what that hateful husband of hers had done to her.

"I mean, can you believe it? Our darling Sarah suffering at the hands of such an awful man. We were heartbroken, weren't we Barty?"

Barty agreed whole heartedly. "Caroline offered to fly over and look after her, but she wouldn't hear of it. She said she couldn't bear to be the reason Caroline was separated from her horses! Lovely to her bones, she is."

"But," Caroline whispered conspiratorially to Henry, "you mustn't tell her, it's a secret. We're going to England soon! Barty has work in London for a few days. I'm going to tag along and then once he's finished, we're going to take a trip to Cornwall. I'm going to tell her as soon as we arrive in London!"

Henry smiled warmly at Caroline; he just couldn't help but like her. She positively oozed kindness and happiness. And Henry knew he was very lucky to have both Barty and Caroline as his friends.

The next morning, Caroline hugged him tightly when the car arrived to take him to the airport. "Send our love to Sarah," she gushed, before finally releasing him. "And remember, not a dickie bird about our surprise arrival!"

On hearing Sarah's name, his heart skipped a beat. By this time tomorrow, he would be with her and would be able to hold her in his arms again. Waving goodbye to the Coopers, Henry eagerly climbed into the car, keen to get going. Sarah was waiting for him.

Arriving in England, he was pleasantly surprised to be met with a clear blue sky and bright sunshine. He took it to be a good omen for his stay in Cornwall. Although Barty insisted that he would organise a car for his journey to Cornwall, Henry had politely declined. He would need his own transport whilst on leave, especially as Sarah still did not have a car! So he had organised a hire car for the duration. He was planning to explore the county that Sarah now called her home, and he hoped that Sarah might accompany him on some of his trips.

The sun was beginning to set when he saw the sign telling him that he had crossed over the border from Devon and was now in Cornwall. Checking his sat nav, he saw he only had an hour and a half to go before he reached the north costal village where Sarah worked and lived. Anticipation and excitement were building within him with each mile his car covered. He checked his watch. She would be leaving work now. He smiled to himself. He could picture her kissing Nicholas on the nose before assuring him that she would see him the next morning. Then she would put her battered rucksack on her back and casually stroll down the mile long country lane to her cottage. Just as she did every evening. Her routine gave him comfort when he was away from her. So many years spent travelling from port to port and in different time zones meant he could convert his time zone to Sarah's with barely a second thought, so wherever he was in the world, he always felt connected with her.

Henry held his breath when he turned down the familiar country lane signposted Elderberry Riding School. *This is it!* And in what seemed like no time at all, he was pulling his car to a halt in Sarah's driveway. As soon as he stepped out of his car, Sarah flung her front door wide open.

"Henry! You're here!" She came tumbling down her crazy paved foot path and launched herself into his arms.

"Hello Sarah," he whispered into her ear, and he held her tightly to him.

"Come in, quick quick," she said, releasing herself from his embrace and ushering him inside. "Supper is ready, I don't want it to burn!" And then she scuttled off into the kitchen like a mini whirlwind.

Sarah still did not have a kitchen table, although if she did get one, Henry wondered where she might put it! The huge sofa dominated the tiny room, and as Sarah didn't seem in the least bit perturbed about her lack of a table, Henry wasn't bothered either. Sarah dished up her home-made chicken and mushroom pie with fresh vegetables on the side and carried the plates on a tray. Settled side by side, Henry thoroughly enjoyed Sarah's delicious pie in her homely, cosy cottage. For pudding, Sarah produced homemade apple crumble, with buckets of custard, explaining that Tia had given her the apples from her little orchard at the yard.

"I'd like that one day," she told Henry. "My own fruit trees in my garden, and free-range chickens so I could have fresh eggs for breakfast every day! And a cat. I'd definitely like a cat. They make a house so homely, don't you think?"

And Henry agreed. He could picture Sarah curled up in front of a roaring log fire, lost in the world of one of her books, and her little cat curled up beside her. And he thought how lovely it would be if the cosy home he pictured Sarah in, was also his home.

"And a library!" he added. "Every house needs a decent library."

"I almost forgot!" exclaimed Sarah. "I got something for us."

Henry revelled in the way she said 'us.' He felt the hairs on the back of his neck tingle at the thought of him and Sarah being an 'us,' and a 'we.'

"*All things Bright and Beautiful*," she announced, handing him a book. "It's the James Herriot sequel to the one you got me! I thought we could read it together."

As he looked at Sarah's beaming face, her eyes sparkling with excitement about the book, he couldn't think of anything he would like more, than to curl up on the sofa and read with her.

Sarah

Sarah was enjoying her morning off. After her relaxing lie in, and still in her pyjamas, she was sipping her hot chocolate and munching on her breakfast toast, when she heard the gentle thud of her mail being dropped through her letter box and landing on her mat. A large white envelope had arrived. Sarah stopped chewing and stared at it. *Is that what I think it is?*

She dropped her toast, no longer feeling hungry as her eyes feasted on the envelope. Padding over, she scooped it up and fondled it with it in her hands. *I'll only know if I open it.* Composing herself, she counted, *one, two, three...*then she ripped it open, pulled the contents out, and stared at the paper. Her eyes greedily scanned the words, soaking the information up as fast as she possibly could. There in black and white was her divorce document. She hastily flicked through the wedge of papers, and there at the end was the space for her to sign her name. She gasped when she saw Julian's signature. It was silly really; she knew he had signed it first. But to think that he had held this exact piece of paper, just like she was now, made her feel nauseous. Any connection with him made her physically wince. She just wanted for it all to be over. To be rid of him. And now, once she signed this piece of paper, she would be.

She fumbled around on her kitchen counter looking for a pen, and then it was time. With shaking hands, she signed her name. And just like that, she was free. She had to send the papers back to her solicitor for him to deal with the final legal side of things, but with both of their signatures, it was done. Relief swirled through her veins with the realisation that Julian was well and truly in her past, and she would not let him haunt her future. She placed the signed paperwork into the self-addressed envelope of her solicitor, sealed it down firmly, and said aloud, "Goodbye, Julian."

Sarah positively skipped down the country lane to the yard, thoroughly enjoying the first day of her singledom. She spent her morning pampering Nicholas, then after encouraging the reluctant Dash away from his grass and on to the yard, she busied herself getting Nicholas and Dash ready on the yard. It was her first day off since Henry arrived six days ago and so far, they had settled into a nice routine. During the day, when Sarah was at work, Henry took himself off to explore Cornwall, and in the evening, they would share supper at her cottage then enjoy reading together.

Sarah didn't like to admit it, but there had been a little niggle of doubt about Henry coming to Cornwall. She had worried that she might have to 'baby sit' him. His work was so all consuming when he was at sea, she was concerned that he wouldn't know what to do with all of his spare time and that she might have to fill the void. And as much as she had been looking forward to his arrival, she knew that her work must come first, especially after all the kindness Tia had showed her with regards to the Julian situation and her unexpected time off work. She was determined to prove herself and show she did not take time off work lightly. She was a hard worker and could be trusted implicitly to do her job, without exceptions.

And thankfully, her doubts had been unfounded. Henry seemed perfectly capable of entertaining himself, and not once had he requested more of her time than she could offer. And even after learning that today was her day off, he still did not push for her company. But she noticed a twinkle in his eye when she had invited him to join her for the day, and he eagerly agreed to meet her at the yard at ten o'clock in the morning.

Nicholas was looking his usual handsome self. His coat sparkled from his morning groom and his regal head was held high, alert to the jumping lesson that Tia was teaching in the nearby sand school. Dash, on the other hand, looked like a huge, slightly frumpy cart horse next to the gleaming thoroughbred. He was a big lad, 16.3 and solid as a rock, pie-bald in colour with a thick shaggy mane which was permanently skew whiff, as was his bushy tail. But his temperament could only be equalled by that of a saint. The big horse had a heart of gold and his job on the yard was to take care of the inexperienced riders, which he succeeded at each and every time. Beginners also suited his naturally docile and somewhat lazy personality. There wasn't much in the world that fazed Dash. His even disposition gave Sarah and the other yard girls complete confidence that whatever they met whilst out on a hack, be it tractors, motorcycles, even the odd ice cream van, Dash would simply just walk on by, completely unruffled. Speed was not really his thing either. The large open space of beach that excited many of the other horses with the thought that they would go running, did not give him any such ideas. Dash was after an easy life. Standing for hours, munching on his hay net whilst being groomed and adored by the Saturday pony club girls, and having pink ribbons tied in his mane was what he was all about. Everyone at the yard adored the gentle giant.

Sarah had tacked both of the horses up and was just placing the picnic into Dash's saddle bags when Henry arrived. She smiled and waved, beckoning for him to join her.

"Henry, meet Dash! He's going to be your ride for the day!" she explained.

She watched Henry hold out his hand for Dash to sniff in greeting. The big gelding turned his sleepy head, gently snuffled his hand, then promptly fell back to sleep.

"I thought that since you enjoyed your ride so much in Thailand, we'd take the horses down to the beach for a picnic!" Sarah said eagerly.

She noticed that Henry looked a little bit nervous, but he met her smile and agreed that it sounded like a great idea.

"Dash will look after you. I'm afraid he only has one speed, so I hope you don't want to go faster than a snail's pace!" She noticed that her words had the desired effect when Henry relaxed his frame and patted Dash affectionately on his neck.

Sarah and Nicholas took the lead, with Dash and Henry ambling along behind them as they followed the single file track from the yard that would lead them to the beach. The clouds overhead were grey, and there was a slight chill in the air, but the weather did nothing to detract from the joy she felt at having Henry with her. Never in a million years would she have thought that she would be horse riding in England with the captain today. That awkward first day when they met outside the Spanish riding school had given her absolutely no idea about how their story would unfold.

The track began to widen as they reached the sand dunes and Sarah encouraged Henry to ride up alongside her, and together, side by side, they sedately rode along the beach. They followed the water's edge, and Sarah enjoyed listening to the Cornish waves crashing on the beach.

"How are you getting along with Dash?" asked Sarah.

Henry grinned at her, then replied, "He's surprisingly comfy! Thank you for lending him to me. It's really nice to be able to step into your world and see your work for myself. You know all about my job! It must be a real sight to see a herd of galloping horses across the beach when you're escorting the holiday makers on their beach rides."

"Oh yes!" agreed Sarah. "Sometimes there can be up to fifteen of us galloping flat out over the beach… Well" she chuckled, "not all of us are going flat out!" she said, pointing to Nicholas. "I have to rein him in a bit, Tia gets a bit worried that we might leave someone behind because he's so blimmin' fast! So, Nicholas and I only really hit fifth gear on my days off!"

"It must be a wonderful feeling to just let go like that. You must have to have so much trust in the horse!"

"There is no other feeling like it in the world. I can give you some lessons if you like? The sand school will be empty in the evenings after work, I'm sure Tia won't mind." And she finished with, "I reckon I can have you cantering across the beach by the time your leave is up."

Sarah watched him mull her offer over in his mind, and was secretly thrilled when he replied, "Ok! That sounds like fun. Thank you."

The grey clouds overhead were refusing to budge and the wind was beginning to pick up, so Sarah guided them off the beach and over to the slightly more sheltered dunes for their picnic stop. Sarah tied the horses to the wooden post Tia had put there years ago for picnics with her own horses, and with the wind blowing, she pulled out the rug and picnic. She and Henry manhandled the rug into position together before swiftly sitting down on it for fear of it blowing away.

They tucked into door-stop-wedge-sized ham salad sandwiches, and Sarah was grateful that she had decided to pack a flask of tea. The steaming drink brought them both some much needed warmth from the biting sea air.

Sarah looked at Henry; his usually well-kept hair was all messed up after removing his riding hat and he was animatedly talking about Dash. And Sarah secretly hoped that horses might be something that they could share, just like they did books. She was already looking forward to giving him some lessons. She noticed how calm he was with Dash, and how gentle his hands were when attempting to give direction to the horse. He had a natural kindness towards animals, and although he still appeared intimidated by the horses, she felt that the more time he spent with them, and the more confidence Dash instilled in him, over time he would feel secure in their presence. She would be true to her word. She and Henry would enjoy a safe, steady canter along the beach before he went back to sea. And she thought privately to herself, *he's going to look super handsome riding along that beach once I've sorted his posture out!*

Sarah brought herself back into the conversation with Henry, instantly agreeing that his first couple of lessons could be with Dash. But she also mentioned to him that if he wanted to get out of first gear, the loveable Dash was not the man for the job! And she promised that she would find him an equally well-mannered horse to progress with.

Sarah felt her pulse quicken when Henry quietly changed his position on the rug. He was now leaning towards her, and she could feel the comforting warmth from his body sheltering her from the wind. Trying to control her breathing, she stayed where she was, perfectly still apart from the odd involuntary shiver from the cold.

"You're freezing," announced Henry. And in one smooth movement he pulled her into his arms. Her spine tingled as he gently rubbed his hands up and down her back to warm her up, then slowly, he pulled away from her. His bright blue eyes were softly looking directly into her own, and in the next moment, she felt his warm lips meet hers as he kissed her. It was not like the first kiss they had shared before he left for Australia. They had grown to know each other so much more since then, and this time, he kissed her, deeply, passionately, and she knew that his feelings for her equalled her own for him.

Nestled in the sand dunes, under the misty grey clouds, cocooned in Henry's arms, Sarah rested her head on his shoulder and thought, *there is no one in the world I would rather share this moment with.* And she wondered if she could bear to be parted with him, because no matter how much she knew she would miss him, and how much her heart ached to be with him, he would, in the not-to-distant future, be returning to his life at sea.

Henry

Henry was sitting in his car, lost in thought as he gazed upon the Cornish mist casting an eerie glow over the barren moors. He was watching the wild ponies graze. Six weeks into his leave and his time ashore was not like it had ever been before. He usually enjoyed the first two weeks. His mind and body needed time to decompress after being alert and focused for so many months. But once the novelty wore off, of lazy mornings and idling his time away in book shops or taking entertaining day trips, the lure of the sea soon sparked up inside him. He had few friends; that was the one downside of the job. He'd kept in contact with some of his school friends, and he usually visited Jennifer, his mother's oldest friend, when he was on leave, but other than Martin, he just didn't have the time to dedicate to friendships. He had learned how things were going to be very early on his career, and he was prepared to make that sacrifice. He was prepared to be a lone wolf in order to achieve his goal. And naturally being a solitary man, it had never been much of a hardship. But now, being with Sarah, submerging himself in her life, and the mystical wild depths of Cornwall, he was beginning to form a bond with the place. As a natural wanderer, this was a very unusual feeling indeed.

And so, he had visited a rather highbrow sailing establishment during one of his day trips. They were advertising for a navigation and nautical lecturer, and they nearly tripped over their own feet on hearing how highly qualified he was. They had offered him the job on the spot, but Henry knew he could not make such a decision so quickly. He assured them that he would give them his answer soon. And after two weeks he still could not commit to a decision. But what he had committed to, whole heartedly, was Sarah. The only question was, would she want to commit to him?

Henry's phone bleeped, pulling him out of his thoughts and alerting him to a message from Mrs Milly Willows. Mr and Mrs Willows were the owners of his holiday cottage, which was situated right next door to their own home. They were a friendly couple and Henry had struck up rapport with them after a little tortoiseshell cat kept appearing in his cottage. About an hour she stayed, curled up amongst the comfy throw cushions on the sofa, and after her snooze, she disappeared again. Mrs Willows had chuckled good-naturedly and explained that she belonged to her, her name was Cordelia, and she was probably just getting some much-needed peace and quiet from her three boisterous kittens! She had then ushered him into her home and proudly showed off the three adorable fluff balls. She scooped one up and announced that she would be keeping her, the only girl of the trio. Her daughter would be taking the other, and unfortunately, Mr Willows had put his foot down, and she must find a home for the third. And that is when a light bulb had lit up in Henry's mind and he had found himself asking Mrs Willows if he might be able to purchase the kitten for Sarah. Mrs Willows had asked many questions about Sarah, clearly trying to make sure that her beloved kitten was going to a good home, but after Henry had assured just how wonderful Sarah was, and that her whole world revolved around horses, Mrs Willows seemed satisfied. As soon as the kitten was old enough to leave his mum, he could take him to Sarah.

I'm home!

Pop over whenever suits this evening.

Kitty ready and waiting for you.

Milly

His plan was about to come to fruition. He had even managed to get Tia on her own and tentatively asked if Sarah would be allowed a cat in her rented cottage. Animal-loving Tia had beamed at him, thrilled at the idea, as she herself had four cats. And so, with everything in place, he started up his car and made his way to Mrs Willows' house.

It took him close to half an hour to leave Mrs Willows' house, with all of her fussing and worrying, but he reminded himself how hard it must be for her to say goodbye, and how thoughtful she had been by organising everything for the kitten. Since he himself was unsure what exactly a kitten might need, Millie had taken it upon herself to do it for him. He had given her a handful of notes and she assured him that she would take care of everything. And she had. Henry couldn't believe how much stuff one tiny creature needed! After Millie's final goodbye, she safely tucked him into his carry box, and handed him over to Henry. It was time for him to meet Sarah.

Henry was relieved to see the light on in Sarah's cottage, assuring him that she was home. He carefully unbuckled the carry crate, looked at the bewildered looking kitten and told him that he'd arrived at his new home. Sarah flung the door open before he had reached it, welcoming him warmly, announcing that toad in the hole was for dinner. And then she stopped in her tracks.

"What have you got there?" she enquired, curiously eyeing up the carry box.

"Best we go inside first," he replied, ushering her in, keen to get the kitten out of the chilly evening air.

A timid meow came from inside the crate when Henry placed it on the sofa, giving the surprise away to Sarah.

"Is that a kitten?" she said eagerly.

"It is! He's for you."

"You got me a cat! Oh, my word! Thank you so much," she squealed, jigging up and down on the spot, before wrapping her arms around him in a bear hug.

"Let's get his things out of the car and then you can meet him!" It took both of them to carry his bed, scratching post, toys, feed and bowls into the house. And then, when the door was securely closed behind them, Sarah tentatively opened the crate and lifted out her bundle of fluffiness. The little kitten was tortoiseshell, just like his mother, and he had a fluffy white belly and four white feet.

"Isn't he just the most adorable little thing! I think I'll call him Thomas! He looks like a Thomas, don't you think?"

Henry nodded in agreement and contentedly watched Sarah fuss over Thomas.

"You'll keep me company when Henry goes back to sea!" she announced, her eyes shining brightly at the kitten.

And Henry sensed that if ever the time arose to mention his job offer, it was now. Clearing his throat, he quietly said, "But what if I didn't go back to sea?"

"What?" said Sarah, taking her eyes off the kitten and looking directly at him. "Why would you not be going back to sea?" she asked with querying eyes.

"I've been offered a job in Cornwall. Teaching navigation at a sailing college."

"But I don't understand, why don't you want to go back to sea? I thought you loved your job?"

"I do Sarah," he said tentatively. "But I love you more." There, he'd said it. It was out in the open. Now all he could do was wait and see what Sarah thought about it all.

Cradling Thomas in her arms, she got up from the sofa, reached up on her tip toes, and kissed him.

"I love you too," she whispered. "But if you think I'm letting you give up the sea you've got another thing coming," she said rather crossly.

"But I thought that's what you might want. For us to be together like a regular couple. I thought the months away might be too much for you."

Looking him square in the eyes, she replied, "Would you ask me to give up my life here? Would you ask me to give up Nicholas?"

"Of course not," he stuttered. "Horses are your life."

"Exactly!" she said, nodding determinedly. "So why on earth would you think I would ask you to give up your passion? Your life?"

Henry looked at her, trying to take in everything she was saying, and before he had chance to reply, she ploughed on. "I do love you Henry, I honestly, truly do, but there is no way that I would give up my job here, and absolutely no way on earth that I would give up Nicholas, even for you. So, for me to ask you to give up the sea would be ridiculous. More than that, it would be downright unfair."

"So, you want me to go back to sea?" he asked.

Her face softened. "Henry, I want you to do what you want to do. Relationships are about accepting people for who they are. I know everything about your job, and I still fell in love with you! We can make this work; I know we can. Plus," she continued, holding up her new friend, "I have this little chap to keep me company whilst you are away. I thought that was the reason you got him for me?"

"I got him for you because I knew he'd make you happy."

"And he does, very much so! Now, do you want to take the job in Cornwall, or do you want to go back to sea?"

Henry and Sarah talked. They talked all the way through their toad in the hole and syrup sponge pudding. And they talked contentedly into the night on the sofa, with Thomas clambering around all over them. They discussed every angle of the job offer, and everything he loved about being at sea. And in his heart, he knew he wanted to go back. With Sarah's encouragement and honesty, he was able to put his fears aside. She had instilled faith in him. Faith that their relationship could flourish, even with him spending so much time away from her.

Sarah was resting her head in the crook of his shoulder with Thomas snoozing contentedly on her lap, and he knew, without a doubt in his mind, that Sarah was the woman he wanted to spend the rest of his life with.

"Sarah. Sarah, will you marry me?" he asked, his heart beating ten to the dozen in his chest.

She turned awkwardly to face him, doing her best not to disturb the sleeping cat. "Yes," she whispered, her eyes dancing in delight. "I would love to marry you!"

He leaned over and tenderly kissed her, lingering so he could inhale her familiar citrus scent. *She said yes!*

"We'll be a little family," Sarah announced happily. "You, me, Thomas and Nicholas."

The word family washed a wave of contentment right over him. His family. The family waiting for him. The family he would think about when he was far away out in the middle of the ocean, and the family he would come home to. And with that in mind, he felt it. The familiar fizz of the sea calling him. The tingle of excitement of the adventures that were to come. It was back. And he knew that he would not turn his back on her call again, and that Sarah would never ask him to.

Sarah

Sarah was carefully watching Henry and Giggles in the sand school. After three lessons on the reliable Dash, Henry had reluctantly parted with the trustworthy steed, and agreed to ride a more forward-going horse, because quite frankly, getting Dash to trot was far more effort than it was worth! Giggles, on the other hand, was a keen bean. A slightly smaller horse, he was a 15.2 hand chestnut gelding, and although he was strong enough to carry a man, he was also nimble on his feet. Sarah was unsure of his breeding- a bit of a Heinz 57, Tia had explained - but he was as willing to please as a puppy! And after three weeks of lessons on Giggles, Henry was really starting to get the hang of it.

"That's right," called out Sarah. "Now sit tight and ask for canter." And the happy little horse smoothly transitioned up to a steady canter.

"You're really getting it now!" praised Sarah. "See how quickly he responds if you give him the correct aids!" And she watched Henry confidently canter around the school, grinning from ear to ear.

"We'd better call it a day," announced Sarah as the light was fading quickly under the setting sun. "We have to be up early; we have a busy day tomorrow."

Sarah and Henry had kept their engagement to themselves for the first couple of days, both enjoying their private secret and bubble of happiness. But then she had received a message from Caroline. She and Barty were in England! And they would be coming down to Cornwall in a few weeks to visit. Sarah was beyond excited about seeing her friends again, and that is when she had formed a plan. Why not invite Kelly, Kyle, and Martin down at the same time. That way they could tell all of their friends their happy news together. And so, she and Henry had plotted and planned, and tomorrow, they would be holding a party at Tia's house. They had both agreed that her cottage was too small, so they had chosen to share their happy news prior to the announcement with Tia in the hope of her knowing a suitable place to hold the party. Ecstatic with their engagement, she had immediately insisted on holding it at her ample sized farmhouse.

And the party is not the only thing we have to look forward to, Sarah thought smugly to herself, because tomorrow, unbeknownst to Henry, she would be taking him for his first canter on the beach, just as she promised she would. And she couldn't wait!

Henry drove them both into the neighbouring town and they enjoyed a fish and chip takeaway for their supper, under the stars, on the moonlit beach. And after a lingering kiss in his car, Sarah climbed out onto her driveway and waved him goodbye. He had agreed to meet her at six the next morning on the yard. She had told him that was when the party food was being delivered. And she had a little chuckle to herself when he didn't even question why the caterers would be delivering the food at six o'clock in the morning for a party being held at six o'clock in the evening!

At five o'clock the next morning, after a rushed cup of tea and a slightly rushed play with Thomas, Sarah hurried along the lane to the yard. Nicholas and Giggles greeted her keenly when she produced their feed buckets an hour earlier than usual. After a quick groom, Sarah had the horses tacked up just as Henry was pulling onto the yard.

"Are we going riding? I thought the food was arriving?" said Henry, confusion etched on his face.

"That was just a ruse!" giggled Sarah. "The caterers are coming this afternoon! I think you're ready to see what it's like to ride wild and free on the beach! Well, in a safe and controlled manner with me," she finished. Henry's obvious keenness was clear on his face. "Grab your hat then! Let's go."

Nicholas and Giggles plodded quietly side by side along the beach, the morning sunrise bursting through the sky in blushed yellows and pinks.

"Are you ready?" asked Sarah. And after acknowledging his nod in reply, she asked Nicholas for a forward going trot.

Giggles followed suit, his ears pricked, patiently waiting for Henry's cue to pick up the pace. Sarah looked over to Henry. He was focused and completely in control of his horse.

"Let's go," said Sarah, and with a minuscule release of her reins, Nicholas transitioned into a steady canter.

Sarah felt like she was floating on air, riding on top of her majestic horse alongside Henry. It was one of the most romantic moments of her life, and she squeezed her eyes shut, just for a split second, to imprint the view of Henry riding next to her, and the beautiful ocean sunrise she could see between two little brown ears.

The horses naturally slowed as they neared the end of the beach, and after taking a deep lung full of the fresh sea air, she turned to Henry. "Was it as good as you thought it would be?"

"Better!" he exclaimed. "That was so much fun. Thank you, Sarah, I can't believe I've actually just done that! Can we go even faster next time?"

Sarah felt her heart swell with Henry's enthusiasm for riding, and the knowledge that every time he was home, they would be able to gallop along the beach together. For Sarah, nothing could ever be better than that.

"Oh, I'll have you galloping in no time! Don't you worry about that!" she informed him. "We'd better head home, we have a party to get ready for!"

The rest of their day was spent rearranging Tia's kitchen and her two generous sized front rooms, putting up the decorations, unloading the food order and organising the drinks table. They both knew that Barty would be keen to share his cocktail skills with them all. Then it was time to go home to their respective cottages and get changed.

She twirled in front of her bedroom mirror and watched her navy-blue dress shimmer in the light. "Isn't it the prettiest dress you have ever seen, Thomas?" she asked her kitten, who was staring adoringly up at her. It was the same dress she had worn in South Africa, the same dress she had been wearing when she saw Henry looking so dashingly handsome in his captain's uniform, and the same dress she had been wearing the first time they subtly made each other aware of their feelings. And so, she thought it perfectly fitting to wear her beautiful dress at her engagement party. Although this time, she paired it with her new diamond earrings and matching diamond necklace set that she had treated herself to on her first shopping trip all those months ago with Tia. "A girl has to have diamonds," she informed her cat, justifying her huge expenditure.

They had agreed that Henry would get to Tia's at half past five, in case of early arrivals. Sarah was happy to walk. She would wear her trainers and slip her party shoes on when she got there. Kissing Thomas goodbye, she slipped on her battered rucksack containing her shoes, and headed down the lane to the yard.

It was a good thing they decided on Henry being early because when she let herself in through Tia's front door, bang on six o'clock, the party was in full swing. Tia had strewn twinkle lights everywhere, casting her home in a welcoming warm glow, and music was playing softy in the background amongst all the excited chatter.

"She's here!" called out Kelly, racing over to her and enveloping her in a warm hug.

Caroline was next, eager to wrap her arms around her friend and tell her how much she had missed her.

"I can't believe you're all here," exclaimed Sarah. "It is so wonderful for us all to be together!"

After she had hugged and greeted everyone, Barty announced that it was time for drinks! He busied himself at the home-made bar, claiming he had perfected another drink and they simply must try it. When they were all holding his newest creation in their hands, Henry announced that he had a toast to make. A hushed silence fell on the room and all eyes turned on him.

"There is a reason that we asked you all to be here today. Sarah and I have some news. We're getting married!"

The room erupted in congratulatory applause, but before their numerous questions of when, how and where, could be answered, Henry brought the room to silence again.

"When I asked Sarah to marry me, I regret that I was not one hundred percent prepared for the situation. And so," he said, making his way over to Sarah, "this time, I would like to do it properly."

Sarah watched him get down on one knee, in front of all of their friends, then slowly he slipped his hand into his jacket pocket and pulled out a little velvet box. *A ring! Oh, my word he's giving me a ring!*

Henry slowly opened the box to reveal an exquisite solitaire diamond engagement ring. She heard her girlfriends gasp at the sight of it, and she was sure everyone could hear her heart hammering beneath in her chest.

"Sarah, will you marry me?"

"Yes, Yes, Yes, I will marry you," she squealed, as he slipped the beautiful ring onto her finger and planted a kiss on his lips.

The little party cheered and congratulated them both, before Barty announced that it was time for more drinks! Kelly turned the music up and declared it was time for dancing, and in no time at all the eight happy friends were in full swing.

After some energetic dancing, Sarah and Caroline were eating nibbles and gossiping ten to the dozen about their horses, when Caroline nudged her.

"I think a certain chief mate of ours and your lovely boss are enjoying each other's company!" And Sarah followed her gaze to see them talking quietly together, totally engrossed in one another's company, as if they were the only two people in the room.

Sarah returned Caroline's smile, then confided that Tia had not had much luck with men. Her long-term boyfriend had up and left her after six years together, with his secretary no less. Sarah couldn't help but laugh when Tia had told her how pathetically unoriginal it was. She couldn't even be dumped in a depressingly romanticised way. His secretary, she had balked, what a tremendously boring cliché. That had been two years ago, and she had not so much as looked at anyone else since. Sarah knew how wonderful her friend was, and she also knew what a kind, honest man Martin was, and she felt a warm fuzzy feeling inside her at the thought of them both finding happiness with each other.

"I've had an idea!" announced Barty, hushing the room to gain their full attention. "Why don't you get married in South Africa, at our place!" He quickly turned to his wife to confirm that his idea was as amazing as he thought was, and Sarah noticed Caroline smile broadly before nodding at her husband.

"What do you think?" he continued. "Caroline and I would love for all of you to join us at our humble abode for your wedding!"

Sarah looked at Henry for reassurance. He nodded, then mouthed, "I do if you do!" They had not yet talked about where and when they would get married, but something about South Africa, the place where she had felt so happy, might be the perfect place for her wedding. And if all of her friends could join them…

"Oh, what a fantastic idea!" said Kelly.

"Brilliant," said Martin, looking at Tia, nodding and smiling, and Sarah thought, *no doubt hoping to see her again!*

Henry crossed the room and whispered in her ear, "If this is what you want then I'm all for it. But if not, I can have a private word with Barty. Thank him for the offer but explain it's not what we want."

Sarah was so grateful that Henry offered to diffuse a potentially awkward situation for her, but the more she thought about, the more she could picture the two of them, on Barty's private beach, under a magical South African sunset, as the perfect place to exchange their vows. *Yes*, she thought, *South Africa it is.*

All eyes were on her, waiting for her response. "Yes! Barty, what a fabulous, generous idea. We would love to get married at your home!"

More cheering erupted and excitement flowed amongst them all at the prospect of a once in a lifetime trip to South Africa.

Sarah felt Henry's arms wrap around her waist, and he whispered, "I love you," softly in her ear.

Sarah looked around the cosy, atmospheric room, and soaked up the joy and merriment that positively radiated out of everyone. And she quietly noted how very lucky she was. How much her life had changed since she'd had the courage to step away from her miserable, solitary existence, and open herself up to letting people into her life again. And what a wonderful, quirky, lovable bunch of people she had found. Every single person in that room was now her family, and she loved each and every one of them.

Printed in Great Britain
by Amazon